THE ACCIDENT

THE ACCIDENT

Richard Woodman

This first world edition published in Great Britain 1995 by
SEVERN HOUSE PUBLISHERS LTD of
9–15 High Street, Sutton, Surrey SM1 1DF.
This first edition published in the USA 1995 by
SEVERN HOUSE PUBLISHERS INC of
595 Madison Avenue, New York, NY 10022.

Copyright © 1995 by Richard Woodman

British Library Cataloguing in Publication Data
Woodman, Richard
  Accident
  I. Title
  823.914 [F]

  ISBN 0-7278-4777-5

All the characters and events described in this story are entirely
imaginary: any resemblance to real people, living or dead, or
happenings present or past is coincidental.

Typeset by Hewer Text Composition Services, Edinburgh.
Printed and bound in Great Britain by
Hartnolls Ltd, Bodmin, Cornwall.

"Superstition and accident manifest the will of God."

Carl Gustav Jung

Chapter One

Naismith woke reluctantly as though from a great depth, irritated by the naked light that glared from the deck head. The face of Quartermaster Potts bent over him and as Naismith's aching eyes focused on the pink message form, he realised he had been asleep for no more than an hour.

"Oh, for Christ's sake . . ."

"Message, sir."

"Read it."

Naismith rubbed his eyes as Potts read jerkily. The string of figures was incomprehensible to his tired brain, although he grasped that the longitude was well to the west of their present anchorage in the Downs, somewhere down-Channel. His mind fastened onto the nub of the message: *A collision has occurred . . .*

He recalled the dense fog that had persisted throughout the previous day and had given him thirteen exhausting hours on the bridge, a period that had only ended a short time before this unwelcome news. The thought brought him further from oblivion. The fo'c's'le bell was silent, no longer giving out its signal for a vessel at anchor.

"What's the visibility like?"

"Cleared up about half an hour ago, sir. See three or four miles now."

Naismith grunted. That most perverse natural law that ensured circumstances changed for the better, the moment human endeavour had achieved a state when that desired change no longer mattered, appeared to dominate his life as usual. The bell had kept him hovering on the edge of blessed unconsciousness for a long time. He must have drifted off to sleep when it stopped. He sat up and threw his legs over the bunk's leeboard. He tried to concentrate on the message. *One vessel reported sinking. Please investigate and report.*

"Very well. Tell the second mate to prepare to weigh. Let the engine room know and call out the carpenter."

"Let the second mate know, aye, aye . . ." Potts paused, a veiled displeasure in his voice and Naismith remembered his new second officer was a youthful female. He sighed.

"Coffee, sir?"

Naismith nodded. "Please. Thanks."

Alone, he resisted the temptation to flop back into the bunk until Potts returned with the coffee. Another five minutes would be bliss, but the image of collision had lodged in his mind to stir his imagination. He thought of the fog, of the instant of indecision, the sudden doubt followed immediately by a surge of fear as the sidelight of a ship signalled the approaching mass, the sickening crunch and scream of steel, sparking vividly as the two ships smashed together. There would have been a lurch as men were hurled from their bunks, a moment of stunned disbelief then shouting panic as the familiar world disintegrated. The image of water swirling darkly across the deck resolved itself into the carpet pattern of his cabin and Naismith shook himself awake. He rose onto aching legs as Potts returned with the coffee and reached for his trousers. Shambling into the bathroom, he dashed cold water onto his face and stared at the red eyes in the mirror, looking at him from the image of the long, lugubrious face. He was thirty-eight but felt at that moment much older. He dressed unhurriedly, waiting for the rumble of the main engines. His wife's photograph watched him, the straw-blonde hair curling at the nape of her neck in a long defunct style. Her acceptance of his proposal still surprised him eleven years after the event. At three in the morning, he thought, squeezing a worm of toothpaste onto a brush, the body was at its lowest ebb, a prey to doubts and uncertainties, inviting the familiar into the vacuum left by spent energy.

On the bridge Ms Susan Paulin, who had slept before coming on watch at midnight, was cheerfully efficient. "Good morning, sir."

Naismith grunted monosyllabically. He was damned if he was making any sexist concessions. "Go on, tell me the worst."

Second Officer Paulin looked down at the scribbled notes and scattered charts.

"Well sir, there's been an accident, a collision between the Liberian vessel *Wallenstein* (no idea of her tonnage) with a crew of thirty, including two women. The other vessel is the Panamanian ship *Calliope*. It seems she's least damaged, probably her bow into *Wallenstein*'s side. Anyway the latest traffic . . .", she nodded to the wheelhouse radio loudspeaker kept permanently on the international distress frequency of 2182 khz, "indicates the *Wallenstein* is sinking here." She indicated a pencilled cross on the chart. Naismith noticed her hands, slim, the nails neat but unvarnished.

"Uh-huh." He had to admit she appeared very efficient; one could almost forget her sex. But the little pencilled cross to the north and east of Guernsey had a feminine look about it and he was too tired to resist a small wave of irritation. "There?" he asked unnecessarily, peering at the chart.

"Yes, sir," she answered.

"Anything else?" He looked at her grey eyes. They were defensive; she was a new second officer on a strange ship wondering how to handle a tired master in the middle watch, and he was a prejudiced fool refusing to acknowledge a very professional thoroughness.

"Yes. *Calliope*'s standing by and the ferry *Armorique* is going to their assistance. The Guernsey lifeboat has left St Peter Port and the last I heard was that *Wallenstein*'s crew were taking to their boats and life rafts. Oh, and Falmouth Coastguard are MRCC."

Naismith grunted again and picked up the brass dividers.

Susan Paulin anticipated him. "Two hundred and five miles, sir."

"Christ," muttered Naismith; nineteen hours steaming. He looked at the courses that she had already laid off, nodded his approval and gave her a tired smile. "Right. That's fine."

Rubbing the stubble on his chin he moved to the wheelhouse windows as Potts answered the "engines ready" signal from below. The quartermaster moved unhurriedly through the routine of switching off the decklights and Naismith felt his eye muscles ache as they strove to acquire night vision.

The familiar outline of his ship emerged from the gloom. The *Active* lay anchored in the Downs, in

4

company with half a dozen other ships, mostly coasters. He looked at the shapes of the four huge steel buoys chained to the deck, buoys that he had intended to lay at daylight, replacing the rusted and weedy seamarks that had served their time round the southern end of the Goodwin Sands.

Ah, well, he soliloquized to himself, it was not unusual in the Navaids Service to have one's plans shot to pieces by unexpected news.

Forward a torch flickered where the carpenter watched the incoming cable chink over the capstan whelps, looking for the white painted shackles every fifteen fathoms.

Water no longer swirled over the carpets of Naismith's imagination and the doubts about his marriage had receded to occupy their permanent and manageable corner of his mind. He had become professional again; "psyched" himself up, as the young officers would have said. He was no longer a private person.

He thought again of the collision, this time with professional detachment. By the time *Active* arrived on the scene the safety of life would no longer be of paramount importance. All the ship would have to do was check the depth over the wreck and declare it safe for the passage of other ships. And if it were not, then she would lay buoys round it. A routine job: a piece of cake.

Except that it was rarely as easy as that. Passing shipping was usually ignorant of the danger, a danger that was deemed to exist until Naismith pronounced otherwise. At least half of *Active's* resources would probably have to be devoted not to sonar searching, surveying and plotting, but to the prevention of other ships ripping their bottoms out on the wreckage.

He remembered other similar disasters. They so often had the nightmarish quality of the impossible, but Naismith knew they were not. Fate was as capricious as she was dispassionate. Had she not connived at this present incident between the *Wallenstein* and the *Calliope?* Yet he, James Naismith, master of the Navaids – tender *Active* of 1650 gross registered tonnes had brought his ship safely through thirteen hours of dense fog. Was this just the result of professionalism? He thought of the dull hours of staring unseeing into the nacreous day that had faded slowly into night; of listening to the monotonous reports from the changing rota of navigating officers at the radar, of his own frequent inspections of the screen, of the alterations of course and the anxious wait to see the effect; of the moaning siren and the yellow-clad misery of the lookout dripping on the fo'c's'le head. He knew, too, the cumulative effects of the simplest miscalculation. Disaster was the sum of a sequence of small mistakes.

It did not require much imagination to know that a man's luck could run out, that tiredness could blur his judgement and that a misappreciation was both cause and consequence of such human fallibility. That a man who never made a mistake never made anything, was a piece of homespun wisdom that had the permanency of truth.

Naismith nurtured a seaman's fundamental superstitious belief in fate, an attitude absorbed rather than learned, as much part of him as the archaic jargon of his calling and quite impervious to the iconoclasm of the twentieth century.

A sharp, single stroke on the bell from forward indicated the carpenter had hove the fifteen-fathom shackle over the capstan and the anchor would be aweigh at any minute. The steering motor indicator lights glowed a dull green and Naismith moved the engine controllers, watching for the tachometers' responses. Both propellers kicked over and he stopped them again and awaited the rapid bell-ringing from the fo'c's'le that announced the anchor aweigh.

"First course is one-six-five, sir, clear of the anchorage." Susan Paulin's incongruously pitched voice advised him. Reflecting that he supposed he would accustom himself to it in time, he looked at the bridge-wing gyro compass repeater and swung the azimuth ring. He glanced round the horizon visible from *Active's* starboard bridge-wing. The air was still damp and chilly. The bell rang forward. He pushed both controllers halfway down until he heard the muffled thud of the anchor settling in the hawse pipe. The faint cry of "All clear!" came to him from the carpenter.

"Starboard easy."

"Starboard easy, sir. Starboard easy it is." Potts' face was visible in the faint light from the steering repeater. Naismith rang the engines to full-ahead as *Active* began to turn with ever increasing speed. The lights of Deal swung across her stern, the flash of the East Goodwin lightvessel six miles away to the eastward tracked across her bow. He watched the compass card spin in the wing repeater.

"Midships."

"Midships, sir. Midships she is."

"Steady. Steer one-six-five."

"One-six-five . . . steady on one-six-five, sir."

He watched the lights of a small Dutch coaster glide down the starboard side as *Active* completed her turn. A tinny ringing on the Dutchman's fo'c's'le told where he too weighed to resume his voyage. *Active* was nearly up to full speed now, pulling out clear of the anchorage. The grey cliffs of St Margaret's Bay were just perceptible on her starboard bow as she took the tide south and west round the South Foreland.

Susan Paulin's head emerged from behind the blackout curtain surrounding the main radar set and the chart table with its dim, adjustable lighting.

"She'll take one-eight-oh now, sir."

"Thank you. One-eight-oh."

Active steadied on her new course and Naismith crossed the wheelhouse, picking up his binoculars. He swept the horizon ahead. The flash of the South Goodwin lightvessel was to port and to starboard; elevated on top of the cliffs the triple stab of the South Foreland lighthouse came clear of the trees and obstructions to the north of it. Two ferries were crossing *Active's* bow in opposite directions, ablaze with lights which gave the impression that they were additions to the lights of Dover just emerging from the heel of the cliffs. Mere maritime extensions of the M2, he thought with a touch of ironic contempt for the monotonous life of a ferry captain.

Further out, in the south-west going traffic lane, a steady stream of ships, the lifeblood of Europe, sought the wide, diverging shipping lanes of the Atlantic. A concentration of wealth and energy and purpose not seen elsewhere on earth, a lulling evidence of man's desire to trade and coexist. Or so Naismith fervently hoped, for it was not difficult to be lyrical about that chain of navigation lights, reliant as they were upon the corporate skills of his own ship for this stage of their voyages. But it was only a generalisation, with all a generalisation's weaknesses. Out there would be at least one warship, probably Russian, packed

8

with apocalyptic electronics, taking advantage of an old-fashioned, buccaneering darkness to slip through the Strait upon her masters' business. She would be quite unlike the stolid merchantmen who merely proceeded upon their lawful occasions. Naismith disliked naval might, with the visceral reaction of most merchant-trained officers. Whatever those ships were, Naismith thought, how many of them had monitored the warnings now being transmitted by the coastal radio stations about the dangerous wreck off the Casquets? Experience, that great teacher and source of nagging doubt, reminded him that eighty per cent would be oblivious of the possible danger ahead of them. He sighed. The *Wallenstein* had gone down in comparatively deep water. He hoped she lay on her side and posed a threat to none of them.

Active swung round the South Foreland, the brilliant line of lights at Dover nestling in its fold in the Downs. The ancient castle was a floodlit glow above the town. The new course would slide the ship into the south-west bound traffic lane at the shallow angle required by international agreement. A shallow entry into the commercial artery of Europe. A fanciful image. Naismith yawned. It was well past his bedtime.

"Report our intentions to Dover Coastguard, Susan," he said quietly. He could see Dungeness and the red light of the Varne lightvessel. Away to the east of south was Gris Nez. Naismith walked out onto the bridge-wing. The arch of the sky was swept clear of cloud and the stars shone coldly. An airliner winked its way eastward. It was odd to think of all those people dozing away up there.

A westerly breeze was kicking up a slight sea, sharp little wavelets were forming against the Channel ebb.

There was a slight lift to *Active*'s bow as she met the open sea.

Susan Paulin had forsaken the VHF radio and the radar and was staring ahead through the binoculars.

"The vis. is pretty good now, sir," she said.

"Yes. You can give her Full Speed Away and put her on Auto-pilot, course two-oh-oh . . . ." He went on to point out the ships round them and their heads met briefly as they consulted a moment over the radar. There was a faint fragrance from her hair.

"Okay, are you happy?"

"Yes, sir."

"Right then, you have the ship. Don't hesitate to call me if you are at all worried."

"Aye, aye, sir."

He lingered a moment longer. The ancient response in the girl's coolly confident voice niggled him unreasonably. But she was well qualified and had displayed a practical ability during yesterday's fog. She was a proven asset to the ship and it was time he got some sleep.

Naismith dozed during the forenoon as *Active* ran steadily west-south-west, lifting gently to the swells rolling in from the Atlantic. The wind which had freshened during the night had dropped again by dawn and a warm September sun shone down on them. After his lunch Naismith returned to the bridge. There were two or three ships still about, the concentrated traffic of the Dover Strait having spread out, diverged or drawn ahead of them according to size, speed and destination.

He looked at the course on the auto-pilot and then at the last position marked on the chart for 1300 in the second officer's defiantly feminine hand, for it was again her watch. She was leaning on the teak bridge rail, her shoulder length hair ruffling in the breeze. In the wheelhouse Quartermaster Potts silently polished the brass.

Seeing the captain at the chart-table Susan Paulin came in from the bridge wing. "We'll be there about 2200, sir."

Naismith nodded and went into the large surveying chart room abaft the wheelhouse. The plane table was strewn with charts, notes and booklets. The tide tables and co-tidal chart lay on top.

"I've worked out the tides." She produced a sheet of closely pencilled figures which gave the height of the tide over the position of the wreck for every half-hour from 2000 that night. It was a tedious piece of computation but one upon which the accuracy of the forthcoming operation depended.

Naismith bent over the figures, flicking the tide tables over, running his finger down the pages. He picked up a pencil and a jotting pad, scribbling a column of numerals. He referred to the orange and green co-tidal graphs. After a few minutes, finding his results agreed with Susan's, he gave up the cross-checking.

"That looks fine, Susan."

There was no answer. "She," sniffed Quartermaster Potts, suspending his work and holding the frayed corner of an old ensign, "she's on the bridge-wing, sir."

Naismith joined the second officer, leaning companionably on the varnished rail. "Those figures look okay. I've told the mate to get the sweep chains checked this afternoon."

"What d'you intend doing, sir, when we arrive?"

"Well, we'll sweep for the wreck by sonar; at least get a preliminary fix and then sit near it until daylight and keep the cowboys off it." He nodded ahead of them to where a small container ship dipped in the Channel swell and the sunlight caught a flash of spray over her bows.

"You've plenty of sonar paper I take it?"

"Yes, I think so."

"Good. Any more news of our friend?"

"Only that she's definitely sunk, sir, but you'll have seen that signal. Bob got it this morning."

"Yes." While he dozed on his daybed Third Officer Sobey had sent down the pink chit. He remembered its content: *A dangerous wreck is reported in position . . . Ships should navigate with extreme caution in this vicinity . . .*

"That's a Whisky Zulu signal."

"Yes, sir. WZ 2I4 I think."

"Uh huh . . . Hullo Chas, those sweep chains all right?"

Naismith and the girl turned to the newcomer, a powerful, bearded man with a high, domed forehead where his hair had begun to recede. Charles Hobden was *Active*'s chief officer or chief mate. He was usually called *the* mate, a fitting title for a big bear of a man.

"Yeah. Bosun's stretching them out on the boat deck now and young Bob is working a field-day remeasuring them."

Naismith smiled. "You heartless bastard," he said amiably, conscious of Hobden's sudden, almost protective look at the girl. But he made no apology for his language; it had always been coloured by a vivid coarseness, and as second mate of the *Active* Susan was going to have to put up with it. Besides, Naismith thought, the bachelor Hobden's old-fashioned protective attitude to women needed modernising.

Hobden himself grunted gruffly, referring to the third officer's enforced overtime. "It's not my job to be popular . . . By the way sir, I just heard the news on *The World at One*. They mentioned a collision, said it occurred west of the Casquets lightship." The last word was uttered with a weary contempt.

"Well, the BBC usually get some detail wrong. Anything else?"

"Yeah. The *Wallenstein*'s sunk, twenty-eight of her crew were picked up, three drowned and two missing, including a woman." Naismith noticed another glance at the girl. He sensed that the overcoming of his own prejudice was as nothing to the struggle Hobden was having at accepting Susan as part of the ship's company. It occurred to him that despite a considerable resistance to even the notion of a woman on the bridge, the actual presence of Susan was disquieting in other ways. There was something oddly, even endearingly, callow about Hobden's demeanour, as if this big, bluff, fearless man was shy in Susan's presence.

"Poor devils," said Naismith, "did they say who she was?"

"The master's wife, apparently."

"And he got away?"

"Well they didn't imply he went down with the ship."

"Jesus . . ." The three fell silent for a second, trying to imagine what it was like to lose one's wife as well as one's ship. Then Naismith said, "There but for the grace of God . . ."

"Yeah. The *Calliope*'s on her way to Cherbourg. French tug standing by. We might get some pictures on the evening news."

"Yes. Okay Chas, thank you. That'll depend on

whether the bloody television reception's any good, but it'll help if we've a rough idea what we're looking for."

"Okay." Hobden nodded. "I'll go and chase young Bob up." He left them giving a last look at Susan, Naismith noticed with a quickly suppressed smile. He and Susan turned forward again, leaning on their arms on the rail, wrapped in their own thoughts.

Lowering his eyes from the distant horizon Naismith looked down at the rolling hiss of the parted sea as *Active* drove through it. A white plastic bag ran down the side.

"Look at that!" said Susan sharply. They ploughed through a mess of floating rubbish, plastic bottles, discarded cans, a fertiliser bag. Naismith sensed outrage from the girl. "That isn't ship's rubbish."

Naismith smiled to himself again. Susan Paulin was an espouser of causes, judging by some of her conversation at the saloon table. He supposed it was inevitable, given her generation, her sex and her chosen profession. You did not invade a male preserve like seafaring without some pretty strong convictions and a character to match. He stole a sideways glance at her. She was quite pretty in profile, he thought, wondering if it was her attraction that was causing such an obvious turmoil in poor old Chas Hobden's flinty and uncompromising heart. He wondered too what ambition had driven her to sea. He found it impossible to guess, her attitudes seemed so remote from his own simple desire to command a ship.

"What do I call you?" he had asked when she first joined *Active*. "Mrs, Miss or Ms?" he had buzzed.

She had shrugged, two spots of annoyance forming on her cheeks. "Well I'm not married, sir."

She had left the ball deferentially in his court and he had even then made a mental note of her intelligence and sensitivity.

"*Are* you a Ms?" He buzzed again, aware that he was being unfair, provocative and deliberately testing her. She ignored the invitation to mount the soapbox of female liberation.

"That's rather an ugly word," she said quite coolly, and Naismith was aware that he had been made foolish and fallen into an old, and to her, familiar trap. "What's wrong with Susan?"

He had smiled at her then, annoyed with his own pettiness and admiring her handling of her new captain's irascibility. She had smiled cautiously back, the professional ice broken and he was aware that she knew far more about him than he of her.

"Very well," he had said, "Susan it is."

"Do you know, sir," she said now with a sudden anger as *Active* passed through a second patch of rubbish, "I don't think I've looked over the side once since I came on watch at noon without seeing some form of pollution in the water."

"Flotsam and jetsam . . ."

"No, that's almost ecologically acceptable. This has been shore-generated rubbish, hydrocarbon products and that bloody polystyrene foam."

"Yes," he said, nodding, pleased she felt able to let her feelings out and seeing a tacit sanction for his own expletives, "I know. The stuff's so light and catches the sun. We only see a tiny proportion of it passing our track."

Susan warmed ingenuously to Naismith's obvious desire to chat. "God knows where it'll all end. No one I speak to ashore seems to realise the extent of the problem."

"Well, what the eye doesn't see, the heart doesn't grieve over," quoted Naismith sententiously.

He had meant it to sound cynically mature but she seized upon it eagerly.

"Exactly! When Peter wrote an article about it the only reaction he received was a letter from a reader in Fife saying he was an alarmist."

"Peter . . .?" He looked quizzically at her.

"A journalist friend of mine." She turned to face him and there was just that hint of movement about the corners of her mouth, just that questioning uncertainty in her eyes that said the unknown Peter was more than a mere acquaintance. "He's a freelance journalist who specialises in marine matters. He was second officer with Trans-Ocean until they made him redundant," she said a little bitterly, "and he's keen on exposing the abuses of flag-of-convenience owners and their ships." Strangely Naismith felt comforted by the knowledge of this intimacy; as though it reduced her ability to disrupt the passivity of his ship.

"Well," he said referring to his earlier remark and the response to friend Peter's article, "Complacent of Fife's reaction doesn't surprise me, I'm afraid. Most people can't see further than the end of their own noses and if they can they would really rather watch somebody else's problems on the telly than face their own. Besides," he added, suddenly serious despite himself, "collective problems are always difficult to solve, particularly in a complex society when every dog has to wag his tail. It tends to blur the issue, confuses simplicity . . ." He struggled with the metaphors. She did not seem to have noticed.

"That's one thing I love about the sea," she said, suddenly throwing her head back and sniffing the wind that blew over them so that Naismith was abruptly aware of the slenderness of her throat and the body that existed beneath the androgynous uniform pullover, "the way it confers a sense of perspective."

The charm and frankness of the gesture and remark struck him forcibly. It was not so much the appeal of her sex, as the freedom that her sex permitted her. A more conventional second mate, a stolid young man with his feet set on the promotional ladder, would never have ventured it. Almost unwillingly, as if he too, like Charles Hobden, felt subjected to a personal dichotomy, he regretted the latitude he had allowed her.

"It seems so obvious to us," she went on, leaning again on the rail, "that we should curb the dumping of rubbish into the sea, but to people shore-side the sea is so vast that it seems that it is a phobia manufactured by alarmists like Peter."

Naismith shrugged, returning to a more cynical view. "You're quite right, but there are people ashore who campaign against nuclear war, seeing that as the biggest threat, and if that isn't enough they can always populate their nightmares with the effects of chemical warfare, biological warfare, the murder of whales, seals and rhinoceroses or the misuse of pesticides. Then, if they want to really worry about fundamentals, there's the destruction of the Amazon forest which is reducing the planet's oxygen supply. And that's ignoring the problems of vehicle exhaust building up a carbon dioxide layer in the upper atmosphere and the consequent greenhouse effect which will, in turn, melt the polar ice caps . . ."

The two points of colour were on her cheeks again and the muscles in her lips were contracted in a species of anger that was suppressed in respect of his rank. It gave her, Naismith thought with sudden relief, the appearance of a much older and chastened woman.

"It's not something for flippancy, sir! This kind of pollution is the simplest to eradicate and it would dispense with the loss of irreplaceable materials and even create new sources of wealth and employment . . ."

"You sound like the *Sunday Times*," put in Naismith drily, forgetting Peter, the journalist. This time she bit her lip with real fury. "Look," he said soothingly, "I know I'm cynical and even perhaps resigned like those shore-side wallahs I was complaining of, but we all pollute and as for the other lost causes . . ."

"There's no *need* for them to be lost, though," she broke in.

"I *know* that!" he snapped, "But in my opinion the bloody politicians will contrive to send us all to kingdom come without bothering about the litter problem."

She opened her mouth to protest but he went on, "Look, the human race is doomed, Susan, a lifetime of 'sea-conferred perspective' has shown me that. It is only a matter of time before it happens. The method is fairly predictable."

"I don't know how you can say that, having children of your own."

Naismith sighed. "It's precisely because I have children that I see it," he said, looking directly at her. "You don't give a boy a box of matches, tell him not to use them and then show surprise when he burns himself." Her hazel eyes looked almost green with the tears of her emotion.

Christ, he thought in sudden panic, surely she is not going to *cry* on the bloody bridge! He turned forward again, stared at the hard blue line of the horizon and subsided into conciliation.

"When I was a boy, just after the war, I was staying on the Isle of Wight. My father took me to sea one day on one of the old paddle-ferries. They used to run trips round the island, I think. It was quite a windy day, I remember, probably no more than a strong breeze, but in my mind it was rather stormy.

"I remember the sea as very green and the sky a mixture of sun and dark cloud. It was very exciting with the old steamer jumping about and the decks wet with spray, I recall that vividly. But what confirmed the day as truly magic was the appearance of porpoises and dolphins leaping about the ship."

"Then you weren't always 'cynical and resigned'?" He saw her eyes were hazel again.

"Touché," he replied smiling. "But do you know I haven't seen a dolphin round the British coast for ten years."

She sighed. "'The sedge is wither'd from the lake, and no birds sing'."

"Who said that?"

"Keats, sir."

"Oh."

Chapter Two

In *Active*'s wardroom Charles Hobden lay slumped in a chintz-covered armchair. He was a big man who lost much of his imposing air when not on his feet, and whose similarity to a beached whale seemed emphasised in juxtaposition to the equally incongruous floral pattern of the upholstery.

He was watching the television with a concentration that made him oblivious to everything else, nosing through the interference for more details of the collision. His determination reflected the character that had made him what he was, a single-minded professional. Son of a drifter fisherman he had gone to sea with his father when the herring was still king. But he had quickly realised the limitations of his future. The constant image of his father, a failed skipper whose luck had not held, turned him from speculation in the fisheries to a steadier living in coasters. From the fishing trade he had brought one priceless asset: the ability to sacrifice the personal in the pursuit of success. This objectivity quickly raised him from deck to bridge. He absorbed the knowledge of his profession with a steadiness that committed every fact indelibly on his mind and moulded him into the perfect seaman. He was tireless, experienced and expert; competent and utterly reliable. A man of taciturn silences, his pronouncements, when they came, were too dry for humour, too cutting for wisdom. His intolerance of all matters unconnected with the sea was well known.

A demanding taskmaster to *Active*'s crew, he was respected rather than feared, but his virtues were best appreciated by Naismith who remained always a little awed by him, as though Hobden's expertise persistently levered away at those doubts Naismith harboured about himself.

A declining coastal trade had led Hobden to the Navaids tenders of the British Navigational Aids Service, the authority responsible for buoys, lightvessels and lighthouses round Great Britain and known popularly by the acronym BNAS, pronounced "Bee-nas". Hobden had immediately found an affinity for its arcane facts, its secrets of remote landings, of shoals, rocks, clearing marks and tidal eddies. He became a walking encyclopaedia, an intimidating man in physical appearance with his huge beard and tall frame, and the recondite power of his mind.

Now he lay wallowing contemptuously before a snowy picture of the BBC newsreader perpetrating for the second time what to Hobden was the near-criminal error of referring to the Casquets lighthouse as a lightship.

"If it was football they'd tell you how many warts the centre forward had on his arse," he muttered to himself. But he succeeded in snatching a glance at a still frame of the motor vessel *Wallenstein*.

Seaman Davis knocked at the captain's door and waited nervously. It was not Naismith who made him apprehensive but the weight of the problem that prompted this interview with the captain.

"Come in."

Davis lifted the curtain, entered and dropped it behind him.

"Could I have a word with you, Cap'n?"

Naismith looked up from his desk. He had expected Hobden, and the seaman's face was unfamiliar. He shot a sideways look at the crew list. The new name caught his eye.

"Davis, isn't it?"

"Yeah, Cap'n." Davis' accent was thickly Liverpudlian.

"What can I do for you?"

Davis swallowed awkwardly. "Well, I, er, I wondered if, er, I wondered how long it would be before I got a regular job, like?"

Naismith pushed his chair back. Davis had been engaged as a spare hand to fill a vacancy occasioned by one of *Active*'s regular crew. His future was as uncertain as the weather.

"You are only engaged as a relief, Mr Davis. Although we have a number of relieving seamen to disperse throughout our ships to cover for sickness and injury it would be foolish, and indeed irresponsible of me, to promise you anything in the long term."

Naismith saw disappointment cloud the young man's face. There was a hint of resentment too, and Naismith studied the younger man. Davis was a gaunt figure, burned dark by the tropic sun and about twenty-two or three, Naismith judged, but without the cocky confidence of so many of his generation. The captain guessed at a maturity born of a hard childhood suggested by the flat, Liverpudlian twang. Naismith felt a twinge of compassion, then suspected himself of patronage.

"You are particularly anxious to become established?"

"Yeah, Cap'n, it's me wife, like."

"Your wife?" Naismith replied, a note of exasperation creeping into his voice. Seamen should never marry, he thought for the thousandth time, himself included.

"Yeah. I want to bring her to the UK as soon as possible and I must have a steady job, you know."

"Where is she now?"

"She lives in Santa Maria de los Mayas." The sudden Spanish accent suggested a fluency in the language that surprised Naismith.

"Where?"

"Santa Maria de los Mayas, the capital of Costa Maya."

Naismith was confronted by his ignorance until he remembered a television documentary he had seen recently about the small Central American Republic where a popularly elected government had been overthrown by a right-wing, army-led coup. The cheated peasantry had risen and were engaged in a ferocious guerilla campaign to overthrow the military junta. The earnest BBC reporter had rooted out a few unsavoury facts about suspected American involvement through multi-national corporations and the land-owning monopolies of one or two prominent families. The remote and bitter little war had all the familiar twentieth-century consequences of human greed.

Davis pulled a worn leather wallet from the hip pocket of his jeans. The photograph he held out was better than the usual blurred image carried traditionally by seamen. She was very dark with the high cheekbones and sloe eyes of indian ancestry. The wide mouth smiled beguilingly and the nose was sufficiently Spanish to mark her as beautiful.

"Very handsome," he said, taking the proffered second picture reluctantly. It showed the same young woman, undeniably attractive and holding a small bundle to her breast.

"Boy or girl?"

"Boy."

Naismith handed the pictures back. "Look Davis, I can't make any promises but I'll do what I can. In the meantime I expect you to show me what kind of seaman you are. You must serve six months on a probationary basis, but we *may* be able to keep you in continuous employment. Have you sorted out the immigration problem?"

Davis nodded. "Yeah, Cap'n. I just want the air fare and a stable job to let me get a flat, like."

"I see . . . you met your wife when you were deep-sea, eh?" It was pretty obvious, but Naismith felt a lingering curiosity about the girl, a prurient expectation that she was a bar-girl, the ubiquitous hostess and whore of every waterfront in the world. It was difficult to imagine Davis having the opportunity to meet anyone else.

But Davis grinned. "Yeah, Cap'n. I was a month loading a full cargo of sugar for New York."

"And your wife?" prompted Naismith aware that today his interest in the opposite sex was bordering upon the indecent.

"Juanita is a teacher. We met while I was watch-ashore. The little kids ran all over me when they heard I was from Liverpool. Wanted to play football with me, you know, must have thought I played for Everton, or something . . ."

"Right, Davis." Naismith cut the seaman short. He felt awkward about the whole interview. Ignorant of the location of Santa Maria, oddly disturbed by the girl's beauty and astonished at her profession. His own limitations struck him between the eyeballs. And those children under the palm trees had heard of Everton Football Club! He dismissed Davis' thanks with a curt nod.

"Okay, Cap'n."

Hobden loomed in the doorway. "You address the master of this ship as 'sir', Davis." Naismith winced and saw that mixture of resentful disappointment re-establish itself on Davis' face. The image of a grinning Englishman surrounded by Indo-Spanish children up to whom ran a concernedly smiling and lovely teacher melted before Hobden's uncompromising reality. Davis vanished.

"That was a bit harsh, Chas."

"He's a new man, sir," replied Hobden, as if that explained everything.

"Well, what is it?"

"*Wallenstein*'s about 4,000 tonnes gross, three or four hatches with derricks and accommodation aft. Nice looking ship, I reckon German, built about the middle sixties before they forgot how to do it."

"What was her cargo?"

"Didn't say."

"Nor where she was bound?"

"Er, on passage from Hamburg to Santa something, Central America somewhere . . ."

"Santa Maria de los Mayas?"

"Yes, that was it."

"It's the capital of Costa Maya," replied Naismith a trifle archly, amused that there were gaps in Hobden's knowledge and that he could inflict a measure of revenge on Davis' behalf.

"Oh." The curtain dropped behind the mate and left Naismith chuckling at the fortuitous coincidence.

*　　*　　*

Naismith leaned on the bridge wing rail. The wind was rising again and moaned softly in the stays while *Active* pitched easily in the swell, her motors at slow ahead, a gull or two dipping into her wake. Already the day had died; a curtain of cloud sweeping into the Channel from the west had brought rain as night fell. Naismith paced back and forth across the wheelhouse. Behind the quartermaster Hobden bent over the sonar, and the wheelhouse echoed to the resonating pulse as it lost itself in the vastness of the ocean.

"Nothing?"

"Fuck all." The absurd expression was so apt; part curse, part sense.

"Bugger it." Naismith picked up the VHF handset. "Falmouth Coastguard, Falmouth Coastguard, this is *Active*, *Active*, *Active*, do you receive? Over."

There were a few crackling seconds of hesitation and then back came the West Country accent.

"*Active*, this is Falmouth Coastguard. Channel six-seven."

Naismith responded and shifted frequency. The performance was repeated and Naismith unburdened his mind.

"Falmouth, please confirm again reported position of sunken vessel *Wallenstein*, nothing found in last hour."

There was acknowledgement and a pause. "Chas, re-check our own position, make damn certain no one's made a cock-up."

In the increasing gloom of the wheelhouse Naismith ignored Hobden's hurt look. Sometimes overconfidence was a contributory factor to negligence. Fate had stalked the master of the *Wallenstein* and visited her pitiless power upon the unfortunate man and Naismith's own innate caution made him constantly wary.

The coastguard station came back with confirmation of the same position that they had transmitted earlier and Hobden looked up, nodding, from the chart.

"It all tallies," he said.

"Bugger it!" repeated Naismith and then picked up the handset again and pressed the transmit button. "One last service, Falmouth; would you check with Jobourg Control, I believe they may have an update."

Falmouth acknowledged and Naismith said to Hobden, "The French may have something else. We'll have to go on searching all night. If the wreck's a danger to navigation and some fool hits it, the least we can do is to be looking for the bloody thing."

"Yeah."

"You turn in now. Bob Sobey and I will handle things until midnight. You and Susan can take over until four. We'll box search . . ." He broke off as Falmouth called back. It was a female voice this time, confirming the same position from Jobourg Control. Naismith hung up the handset.

"All right for the bloody coastguard sat in a cosy control room engaged in God-knows-what extra curricular activities . . ."

"All black stockings and . . ."

"*Active*, *Active*, *Active*, this is the fishing vessel *Three Brothers*. Are you still on six-seven, Cap?" The VHF interrupted Hobden's prurience. Naismith snatched up the handset.

"*Three Brothers* this is *Active*, over."

"Yeah, Cap. We heard you talking to Falmouth Charlie George. Are you looking for that wreck?"

"Affirmative. Over."

"We've got the stink of diesel on the wind, Cap. Might be that wreck. Over."

"Where are you *Three Brothers*? Over." Hobden bent over the radar while Naismith waited impatiently. The skipper of the fishing vessel still had the transmit button pressed and the thud of her engine combined with a stage whisper: "Where the fuck are we, Jim?"

"Three echoes to the south-east on the twelve mile range," offered Hobden from the radar.

"*Active*, this is *Three Brothers*. Decca Red H 10.5, Green B 38 dead."

Naismith repeated the lane numbers of the Decca lattice and asked the fishing boat to stand-by while Hobden bent over the chart again.

"That's one-four-oh by eight miles from our present position."

Naismith already had his head over the radar. He spun the electronic bearing marker onto the nearest echo.

"One-three-eight by seven point seven miles. That's the bugger." He picked up the handset again. "*Three Brothers*, this is *Active*. Are you in company with two other boats? Over."

"Yeah, Cap, that's us. Over."

"Okay thanks, old man. Are you still fishing? Over."

"Nope. On our way back to Peter Port. One of the crew is sick."

"Okay, skipper. Many thanks for your assistance. *Active* out."

"It's a pleasure, out."

"All the old-world courtesies, all the old brotherhood of the sea and sod those communications experts ashore sitting on the wrong bloody information," quipped Naismith with some feeling. "You can't beat a mark one nose. Hard aport, Quartermaster." Naismith crossed to the engine controllers and pushed them hard down to full ahead. "Bring her round to one-three-eight."

"One-three-eight. Aye, aye, sir."

Active swung her stern round into the wind and the wake bubbled and swirled out from her revving propellors.

From his bunk Francis Davis stared at the deckhead and fought down the disappointment. The St Christopher medallion rose and fell less heavily upon his naked chest and he felt able to look at the photographs on his bunk shelf. They were his private icons, much larger than those he had shown to Naismith, but the subject was still Juanita; Juanita and her son Carlos Miguel.

Those few incredible weeks in Santa Maria seemed so joyous to him now that he doubted their reality. The poignancy of the memory struck him like a reproach, as though he had been caught indulging in a pleasure reserved for others. A sudden flare of returning anger threatened to turn into tears of miserable frustration as he thought of the recent humiliation. The big, bearded bastard of a mate with that 'sir' business, and the smug, middle-class Captain with his "it would be irresponsible of me . . ."

With an effort Davis calmed himself. "Don't kick against the pricks" he remembered the priest saying, "it was God's advice to St Paul". In the present circumstances the Biblical quote had more than Biblical significance. But it was more difficult to submit now that he had met and married Juanita,

30

now that he had enjoyed the tangible pleasures of love. The vague promises of the hereafter lost their charm. He thought of the marriage of his parents and the comparison only made him more miserable in his longing for his wife.

His drunken, unreliable Welsh father had been compelled to marry by his mother's relatives who sat disapprovingly round the unfortunate girl's pregnancy. The father had stuck five years of matrimony before deserting his wife and son. With his Welsh name and unintended birth he became an outsider to his Liverpool-Irish cousin and a loner among his schoolfellows. He was close only to his mother, a prematurely faded woman to whom life brought no joy and whose only relief had been the departure of her unloved husband. It was both Francis Davis' sense of isolation and his devotion to his mother that had brought about his present crisis. Isolation from his peers saved him from their fate, that of the docks, the shipyards or the dole. For Frank Davis the docks meant the smell of blue water, for above the chimney pots of Birkenhead, the azure funnels of Holt's "China Boats" echoed the tropical skies whence they traded. The smell of exotic cargoes that wafted from their open hatches over the rooftops of the narrow houses that flanked Vittoria Dock was redolent of longing. It was the scent of liberty.

He left home as soon as he decently could and went to sea as a galley boy, not on a Blue Funnel Liner, but a Glasgow-owned tramp. From his father he had inherited a love of words and the ship's library opened his mind as that first voyage opened his eyes. After several months of sending regular allotments home to his mother he was transferred to the deck by an indulgent mate and following a brief, swaggering spell ashore in Glasgow where he lost his virginity and gained a deck hand's certificate, he settled to the sea life.

His mind occupied by reading, his body by the physical effort required at his work and his conscience quietened by his mother's pathetic letters of love and gratitude for his regular allotments, he spent several years in the nearest state to happiness he had yet experienced.

The meeting with Juanita had been idyllic and with his ship chartered to carry sugar and coffee from Santa Maria de los Mayas to New York, his life settled briefly into an unprecedented pattern of wonderful predictability. They were married on his third visit to Santa Maria. The inevitable end of the charter and return of the ship to home waters was to be no more than a brief parting for the lovers. Davis was to return to Santa Maria and settle. His wife's socialist passions awakened in him an inherited Welsh fire. And where the tired old shores of the Mersey had a tragic immutability, as though the mean poverty of its terraced houses were geological formations rather than excrescences of man, Santa Maria seemed eagerly awaiting change. Juanita's life had been given over to the reshaping of young minds accustomed to the acceptance of misery. Soon Davis was as enthusiastic as his wife. But he had to return to the United Kingdom to fulfill his articles and pay off the ship. And to inform his mother of his marriage.

He found his mother already dying the long, lingering death of a cancer. The heel of circumstance ground out the poor woman's life by a final and total indignity. Trapped, he consoled his waiting by applying for an entry permit into Costa Maya. The authorities delayed and procrastinated. Juanita wrote to say that she was pregnant and would have to leave her job. Davis' money dribbled away, his mother's illness was protracted.

Then came news of another kind. A brief hope sprung into Davis' heart. Juanita wrote to say everything would be all right after the old order had been swept aside. There were going to be elections but a reign of terror and intimidation had begun. Juanita's letters became increasingly desperate. The elections, carried out under great difficulties had nevertheless resulted in a landslide for the popular parties, a coalition dominated by the Communists. In a mood of euphoria a government was formed, speeches of rosy intent were made and the peons in the villages went wild with joy. Two weeks later the right struck back. There was a military coup and American built armour rolled remorselessly through the villages and along the tracks that ran beside the waving sugar canes. The cheated peasants took to the hills and jungle to start a guerilla war of ferocious bitterness. Davis received the photographs of Carlos Miguel and his mother just before the junta interdicted outgoing mail.

Davis looked at the pictures again. In the background was the blurred image of a curious bystander. His American steel helmet and machine gun were recognisable.

Torn by worry and indecision, Davis remained in Birkenhead, eking out his savings with odd jobs, as cellarman in the pubs his mother once cleaned and where people remembered her with little kindnesses for her son. He worked as a builder's labourer, rough painter, anything to raise money and contain the mounting rage in his heart.

In the end he knew he was beaten. Juanita feared for her baby and a television documentary lifted the veil a little on what was going on in Costa Maya.

Davis' applications to the Costa Mayan Embassy continued to be turned down. When his mother was eventually admitted to a hospice to die, Davis obtained a post as a relieving seaman with BNAS. He had made his mind up. Juanita and her son must come to Britain. They would continue the fight against Fascism and one day, one day he swore to himself, they would return.

As though this moment of decision was approved of by fate he received a letter smuggled out of the country and posted from Belize. It was a long, passionate and desperate letter and Davis picked it up now from the bunk shelf to re-read it for the thousandth time. Juanita feared she had been deserted, but illegal lines of communication were opened. People could be smuggled out of the country. He *must* help. There were instructions as to how he might write back without fear of the censor.

But it all cost money.

Chapter Three

Susan Paulin lowered the binoculars and reached for the aldis lamp. Her heart was thumping painfully as her apprehension increased. She began sending the two shorts and a long of the morse signal "U", the international warning that a ship was standing into danger. The oncoming navigation lights did not waver. She flashed again then lowered the lamp and, running into the wheelhouse made a blind transmission on Channel 16 VHF.

"This is the British Navigation Service Ship *Active*. I am marking a dangerous wreck, all ships should keep clear!" For the first time in her career she felt her female voice to be inadequate and as the lights remained steady she reached again for the aldis. She was about to call Potts to wake the captain when the VHF crackled with a thick, indeterminate foreign accent:

"What ship is that? What is the matter? Why are you calling me?"

"This is the British Navigation Service Ship *Active*. You are standing into danger . . ."

She knew that on a dozen bridges within a twenty mile radius she would have stirred a dozen middle-watch keepers, but what the hell? Her heart continued to hammer, pumping adrenalin into her blood-stream as the port light shut out and the masthead lights of the oncoming ship separated. The passing ship towered over the smaller *Active* as her bow swung away and they heard clearly the swish of water along her side and the steady thump of her diesel.

Susan Paulin swallowed with relief, aware that she was shaking violently.

"D'you like a coffee Miss?" asked Potts matter-of-factly, but his eyes conveyed a measure of grudging approval at her.

"Yes please."

She watched the accommodation lights and stern light of the strange vessel as it slipped astern, past *Active* as the tender lay at anchor with her wreck-marking lights hoisted. It was the fourth close shave they had had in the two and a quarter hours Susan had been on watch.

She crossed to the sonar and turned the volume up. The trace showed a hard echo on their port quarter and the quick response to the set's pulse was hard and metallic: the freighter *Wallenstein*.

"Thanks." She took the coffee from Potts.

"Bunch of bloody cowboys, eh?" said Potts conversationally, staring at the sonar and dismissing the recent incident with contempt. "Where was *she* bound?" he nodded at the sepia blur on the sonar trace.

"Central America. Place called Santa Maria de los Mayas," she said knowledgeably, passing on information given her by Hobden.

"Oh, yeah. I've been there. In the old Harrison Line, er, the *Academician* I think it were." He chuckled. "The old two o' fat and one o' lean."

"Sorry?" Susan turned the sonar volume down again while they chatted.

"Two white bands on her funnel with a red one between them."

"Oh, I see." They sipped the coffee. "The old man said the new seaman's got a wife and child out there."

"What, Santa Maria?"

"Yes."

"Oh." Potts shrugged. Relief seamen came and went while old quartermasters went on and on. Potts was not on intimate terms with newcomers to *Active*'s mess decks. There were several hundred ports in the world and it was likely that with her crew drawn from so many sources, at least one of *Active*'s crew would have some connection with almost any of them. Any sense of coincidence was thus lost on Potts. Even Susan herself did not regard the matter as intrinsically significant. She had met Peter ashore in Kobe when their two ships were alongside together and from conversation in the saloon she had gathered that during the Falklands campaign *Active* had her own consultant in the geographical progress of the conflict in the person of the cook who had served in the last British whalers to use the old station at Grytviken on South Georgia.

She moved to the wheelhouse windows with her coffee. The radar screen was empty for six miles, with the exception of their departing friend. She wondered why the name Santa Maria had stirred something in her memory and then remembered the television documentary about the guerilla war raging in the country. She wondered what it was like for the new seaman Davis, with a wife and child in a war zone. Perhaps Davis had skinned out and left them, she thought with a feeling of prickling anger at human indifference. It had made her flare up at the refuse polluting the Channel the previous afternoon and she remembered the captain's sniping at her idealism. The recollection only increased her futile anger. She was mature enough to see how her enthusiasm might seem ingenuous to men, particularly men looking for indications of the weaknesses of her sex. But she felt the righteousness of her point of view with a female certainty, secure in the knowledge that unless more people inclined towards her view there was little future for the world.

"'Ere, what d'you reckon this is, miss?" Potts recalled her abruptly to reality.

"What's that?" she moved over to the sonar at which Potts was peering intently. Between the transducer under *Active*'s hull and the response from the shattered *Wallenstein*, another echo had appeared. It was dense and shadowed *Wallenstein*'s echo. Susan snapped up the volume. The audio response was hard and resonant.

"It's not fish," she said, "but it's moving." She began oscillating the transducer. The strange echo had very definite edges and was moving to the right very slowly. The trace became blurred as a speckle of spurious echoes appeared together with extraneous noise through the amplifiers. This stopped abruptly and then the echo began to move again.

"What on earth is that?" Susan tried to track the echo which moved swiftly out of the range of *Active*'s equipment.

"Submarine, Miss, if you asks me."

Susan considered the matter. "No . . . dolphins I think, dolphins following the mackerel into the Channel."

Potts sniffed his disagreement. Just like a woman to

think it was bleeding dolphins. He turned to answer the engine room telephone.

"The third wants you, Miss." He held out the phone.

"Hullo Colin, what can I do for you?" She paused and smiled at the engineer's mild impropriety. "Let me rephase that then . . ."

"Don't bother, love. Have you hit that wreck?" Susan could hear the clatter of auxiliaries behind the third engineer's voice.

"What?"

"Have you hit that wreck? We heard some thumps on the hull just now, sounded odd."

"It's wonderful you can hear anything down there."

"I was taking the sea temperature at the time, got my ear pressed up against the shell plating."

"Which side?" asked Susan, a feeling of unease seeping through her.

"Port side. That's the side the wreck's on isn't it?"

"Yes . . . no, it's all right. We're four cables from the wreck." She put the phone down. "Mr Mulliner reckons he heard noises on the hull just now."

Potts sniffed again. "Sub's sonar on us, Miss, then he moved off. Stemming the tide weren't he." It was a statement not a question.

"What the dickens does he want to do that for?"

"Come and have a look at the wreck I suppose. Curious. Probably heard our sonar from a distance and came to investigate. His gear'll be a bit more sophisticated than ours." Potts nodded at the old Simrad set as it churned its coffee grinder mechanism round and round.

"I suppose you might be right," Susan said cautiously, worrying as to whether she should have called Naismith. "Odd sort of thing to do though, isn't it?"

Having offered his opinion Potts was unwilling to make any further concessions to the second officer.

"Odd sort of bastards in submarines," he replied philosophically.

Susan dismissed the submarine, if submarine it was, as an unpleasant intrusion, to be lumped together with those ships she had warned off earlier and best forgotten. They were not very far from either the Royal Navy's base at Portland or the French naval port of Brest. She knew the warships of either nation might be exercising hereabouts. As for other submarines . . . well she preferred not to think about them but she supposed they must be about.

Whether or not the submarine had come to look at the wreck or to identify themselves anchored in such an unusual place was none of her business. Besides, Potts could be wrong, perhaps it was not a submarine . . .

She tossed the worry back and forward, finally resolving to tell Peter about it in due course. He had some useful contacts in the Royal Navy and collected what he called "snippets". She smiled to herself. Dear Peter . . .

"Bugger's back again, Miss."

She was snatched back to reality. Potts was staring at the sonar. The volume had been suppressed again but the instant she saw what Potts' stubby finger pointed at she twisted the control. The trace tracked across the paper, sending a hard, undeniably metallic echo back to them. It disappeared behind the large echo of the *Wallenstein*. They waited for it to emerge from the sector of shadow beyond the wreck. It did not appear again.

Susan pressed the control that altered the angle the

transducer made with the horizontal, simultaneously sweeping it in azimuth. But the submarine had not altered her depth, if submarine it was. It seemed to have gone to ground behind the wreck.

"Sitting on the bottom behind the wreck," said Potts as if reading her mind.

"Do you think so?"

"Yes," said Potts seriously, "I do, Miss. I was a sonar operator for five years in the 'Andrew'. Even on this thing," he tapped the Simrad with an air of having been used to something better, "I can tell a submarine from a shoal of mackerel."

"And d'you think it's odd that he's settled there, with the wreck between us and him?"

"Yeah. Those blokes down there will have heard us pinging on their passive gear. I doubt that their own sonars will have been picked up by us very clearly since they are probably not on the same frequency and almost certainly knew exactly where we were. With their precision gear they would have kept it well away from us."

"Well we've hardly made a secret of our presence here have we? If the ships on the surface were as knowledgeable as those underneath . . ."

"Ah," said Potts, suddenly, "maybe the ones on the surface had women drivers, Miss . . ."

Susan looked up sharply at the Quartermaster's laughing face.

"Don't be horrible, Mr Potts, you know that last one was a man."

"Could have been the skipper called to the bridge by his second mate." Potts made the rank sound like some gradation in the seraglio of a Turk.

"If," said Susan turning again to the sonar, "if that is

a submarine, d'you think he's hiding from us? I mean if he's a British submarine . . ."

"Look Miss, submariners always act suspicious, it's part of their training. They just love hoisting the Jolly Roger, the British ones the most. They're trained to be bloody pirates."

"Brainwashed more like," said Susan angrily. "I'd better tell the captain."

Eight hours later, as the third rain squall of the morning swept up-Channel, Naismith had forgotten about the submarine. He had in any case not seen it and matters of hearsay at three-thirty in the morning make less impact on the mind than the annoyance at having been unnecessarily woken. He stared now at the motor boats, dipping and rising on the waves as they quartered the wreck searching for "peaks" with their little echo sounders. At the radar, the display switched onto the quarter mile range, the tireless Hobden patiently vectored the boats back and forward over the position of the *Wallenstein*. From time to time, wind and tide swept them off their target and Hobden, aligning the radar bearing cursor and variable range marker with the information from the sonar, conned them back over it.

"There'll be a lot of aeration under those boats," muttered Naismith. The rolling of the big wooden launches would not make the results on their echo sounder traces very accurate, but it was the best they could do in the circumstances.

"*Active, Active*, Number One boat. Over."

"Go ahead. Over."

"We've got some good echoes over the hull and superstructure, sir. I'm not sure about mastheads though. There is one thing we've found; several heavy mooring ropes trailing up to the surface. As the tide gets away they are dragging underwater but you can see them about three feet down. Over."

"Okay." Naismith paused. Sobey had been out there for three hours and the presence of those ropes justified all *Active*'s actions as a wreck marker since her arrival on the scene. It would be best to recall the third mate, assess results and give the boat crews a break."

"Okay," he repeated, "return to the ship, we'll pick you up." He waited for the acknowledgement, put the handset on the hook and addressed Hobden.

"Pick the boats up, Chas, we'll get Bob Sobey up here and see what he's got. Don't like the sound of those ropes though . . ."

"No, some idiot will foul them with his screw . . ."

Naismith nodded. "Yes, Sod's Law."

Hobden called for the davit crew to stand-by to hoist the boats. Naismith bent over a piece of paper on which the crude outline of a ship was drawn. They had received some information about the *Wallenstein*. Meant to be reassuring it had not allayed Naismith's fears. If the ship had gone down on an even keel in the depth of water they were in, given the height of her mainmast from Lloyd's register, there *should* be little danger to shipping. If she had not yet settled, she might still move, one end lifted by air trapped in the hull, and present a very real danger. However the close monitoring by the sonar since their arrival had indicated there seemed little danger of this and Naismith was almost totally confident that the wreck was firm on the bottom.

However, the mooring ropes presented a problem. They would be thick polypropylene and very tough, floating up to the surface in still water and pulled under by a flowing tide as Sobey had reported. It was possible they might inflict a lot of damage on a vessel's propellor or even perhaps her tail shaft. To this certain danger there was added the risk of the wreck being an obstruction to trawlers fishing either with bottom or pelagic trawls. The mackerel were running and until *Wallenstein*'s ruptured hull had been charted through official Notices to Mariners, it would be prudent to assume the wreck was a danger.

A dripping Sobey appeared on the bridge, his yellow oilskins running with rain and spray.

"Hullo, sailor," quipped Hobden, holding out his hand for the soggy echo sounder traces and handling them like the Dead Sea scrolls on the chart room table.

Half a dozen echoes of the hull showed up, peaking thirty metres below the surface with some hard echoes dotted about higher up. Sobey pointed at them.

"They could be the ropes, sir. But they could be almost anything. We were bouncing about a fair bit."

Naismith nodded then looked out of the wheelhouse window. "The weather's not improving. If we're going to lay a buoy on the wreck I'd say we've left it too late today."

"Yeah." Hobden agreed.

"Work out the reductions on those soundings, Mr Sobey," Naismith said, suddenly formal. He turned to the mate. "Chas, there's no way I'm taking *Active* over the wreck until those ropes are removed. We'll have to get a diver to cut 'em away. We can't get a 'least-depth clearance' until then and with this swell running getting a buoy up out of the hold will be risky. I'll get a signal off suggesting we lay an east-cardinal on the thing and as soon as we get confirmation the lads can start painting the emergency buoy in the hold."

"Aye, aye, sir. Let's hope they don't keep us waiting. In the meantime we continue to mark it with the ship?"

"Yes." Naismith reached for the green signal pad and began to write.

Uncharted wreck presumed cargo-vessel Wallenstein located in position 49° 39.80' North 03° 08.60' West. Mooring ropes floating on surface prevent chain sweeps being made with ship. Motor boat survey indicates probable least-depth in excess of thirty metres LAT in surrounding depths of sixty three metres LAT. Consider danger to navigation until ropes removed. Recommend establishment of east cardinal buoy one hundred metres east of wreck. A diver is required to clear ropes. Remaining anchored as wreck marking vessel. Signed Naismith.

Sobey emerged from the chart room. "I reckon the least-depth is thirty-three metres, sir."

"Right, that'll do for now." Naismith handed the signal to him. "Send that off on the telex. The sooner we get an answer the better."

Chapter Four

The wind freshened as night fell. *Active* pitched as her head rode to the west but as the tide turned she swung beam on and rolled uncomfortably, wind and tide in equilibrium, holding her hull athwart their twin forces and forcing her crew to sleep in fits and starts, her watchkeepers to lurch from hand-hold to hand-hold. Squalls of rain hissed across the black water as it sloshed at her hull, the tide-induced upwelling roiling smoothly to windward under her. It was a night of fairly normal maritime misery; warm sector weather to the meteorologist, thick weather to the seaman.

Only twice did ships approach close, one sheering off of her own accord during the first watch, the second refusing to react to prolonged calls over the VHF radio and ignoring the rain-slashed stab of the aldis light sent by Sobey as he stood in the rain, squeezing out his own discomfort in a meaningless stream of profanity. In the end he had discharged a maroon across the stranger's bow, childishly delighted in the roar of the rocket and the satisfactory white flash and thunderous "crump" of its explosive head.

The ship, like a riderless horse, turned away apparently instinctively and was swallowed up in the gleaming black night. Sobey recovered the shelter of the wheelhouse, his moment of excitement over.

Dawn broke in Hobden's watch, a quiet affair with

little speech between duty officer and quartermaster. It was late in coming, the daylight delayed behind belt after belt of woolly grey stratus rolling up Channel, masthead high. Hobden eyed it dispassionately from the wheelhouse windows, his visits to the radar exactly spaced intervals that measured the passing of the morning watch. The quartermaster pottered about, clearing the coffee cups and ashtrays of their nocturnal accumulations, emptying the rosies and eventually tearing the fly out of an old ensign to buff up the wheelhouse brass. It did not do to remain idle in Hobden's watch. He was a big silent bastard but a bawling out from him was not an experience enjoyed by many.

At exactly twenty-eight minutes past six Hobden turned his eyes on the quartermaster.

"Shuter."

"Sir?"

"Call the hands and ask the bosun to come and see me before breakfast."

"Aye, aye." Hobden turned to the phone on the after bulkhead and dialled the captain.

"Morning, sir," he paused while Naismith woke properly. "Not very pleasant, still raining occasionally, though the worst of it's over. She's beginning to swing back to the flood but there's still a sea running with a swell from the west . . ." He let the information sink in, mentally agreeing with Naismith's exasperated oath.

"No, sir, nothing yet, but I reckon we could land a chopper once we're head to wind. Rise and fall isn't that bad . . . Yes, sir, that's in hand . . . Doubt we'll get a signal before nine-thirty, you know those shoreside bastards . . . Okay . . . Yeah . . ."

Hobden put the phone down. Naismith got paid to

48

worry, he reflected sardonically. The ship's day had begun, aromas floated up from the galley and his own morning coffee arrived, brought by the steward who also wanted the work programme for the day.

"Probably have four extra people for dinner, Oswald," he said to the pale cadaver whose stringy neck emerged from a badly buttoned white jacket. No one knew where Oswald's nickname came from, only that it was as eternal as his pale face which had served officers of a variety of ships for nearly thirty years while giving the appearance of imminent demise.

"Helicopter crew and divers," Hobden added by way of explanation at the look of faint puzzlement that crossed Oswald's face. The steward turned and retreated, to be replaced by the bosun, entering the wheelhouse from the bridge wing.

"Morning Bose."

"Morning, sir." The two men seemed to roll inwards towards each other, ending up elbow to elbow on the bridge rail, their eyes inclined not at the emerging horizon, but downwards at the wet foredeck and the ship that was their joint and special responsibility.

Theo Jones was a thickset Welshman with the fair hair and ruddy cheeks of a youth. But his forty-seven years had bronzed his face and given him the complexion of a russet and wrinkled apple. As the backs of the two men leaned together they suggested the companionship of conspiracy, their complementary natures exactly fitting their purpose as mate and bosun; the one big, ursine and immensely final, the other lively, energetic and vociferous. The combination showed its worth in the appearance of *Active*'s upper decks, stores, 'tween decks and alleyways. Naismith counted himself doubly fortunate in these two men.

"East cardinal, d'you say? Ah, that'll be fine. The buoy body's primed already an' just the superstructure to tart up, like."

"Good. I'll get Sobey to put a lamp on test at eight if you can rig it on the test bench for him."

Jones nodded. "Still waiting for the office, is it?"

"Yeah. Usual bloody thing."

"And you want the helicopter deck rigged up too?"

"Yeah. Get that ready right away, then we can forget about it until we get an ETA from the chopper."

Jones moved off when Hobden, recollecting something, called him back.

"What d'you think of Davis, Bose? How's he settling down?"

Jones shrugged. Experience had made him cautious of snap judgements. A man eager to be accepted would oblige for a month or two and then show his true colours.

"He seems all right at present. Good seaman, but we 'aven't done much yet, like. Want me to keep an eye on him, do you?"

"Yeah."

Jones nodded and disappeared. Hobden sniffed, stretched and stared once more into the radar. A small patch of blue sky showed briefly to the westward then it too disappeared. But the clouds were less dense and there were patches on the foredeck where the internal warmth of the ship was aiding the drying process. Hobden began to dream of bacon and eggs and eight bells.

There was something archaic about *Active*'s hold. The smell of it belonged to the last century. Huge coir fenders suffused the ill-ventilated air with their own peculiar aroma of fibre and cork while the locker of tarred spun yarn added a spice to the atmosphere. Lower down, in the cooler air above the tank tops, fleets of heavy mooring chains, each carefully tagged with its length, gave off the sharp tang of superficial rust.

But the hold was not a museum. A huge amount of equipment was crammed into a space designed twenty years earlier for much less gear. Chains, sinkers, snotters, bottle screws, fenders, odd spars, collision timbers, drums of cement, ladders, coils of steel wire, an unused gangway, spare anchors, boat delivery tanks all crowded into the lower hold and lower 'tween deck. There were also lockers containing paint, cleaning gear, brooms, shovels, engine spares, oil lamps, buoy lanterns and a rope store that would not have disgraced a windjammer. There were items that spoke of a new technology; pine packing cases with electronic equipment, curious antennaed fittings to be bolted onto selected buoys and beacons, an odd, emergency and collapsible buoy, a selection of Bruce anchors and coil after coil of shiny orange polypropylene rope. Sitting in the hatch square on the tank top ceiling the huge steel shape of a spare buoy, its red priming being covered with dark grey undercoat by three seamen who clung to its side by any means the anatomy of the *Active* afforded. The smell of drying paint failed to eclipse the other more pungent odours. The drum of *Active*'s auxiliaries filled the air while the chink of chain link on chain link accompanied the ship's easy motion in the seaway. Faint creaks came from the hull and overlying the noise the banter of the seamen filled the echoing space.

"An' then what did yer do?" asked Ordinary Seaman John Ellice, whose curiosity was aroused by the extremely graphic account of Able Seaman Harris' latest sexual exploit.

Harris ceased working his brush and looked at the younger man with affected astonishment. "Well I give 'er one, you daft bastard," he said, his eyes wide with mock surprise. Harris looked at the third man, as if seeking comradely support from one of equal experience.

Frank Davis painted steadily on. There had been a time when he regarded women with that casually detached contempt one has for a necessary convenience. But that had been before he had met Juanita. And just at the present time he did not wish to be reminded of her, preferring the monotonous comfort of the job in hand. He avoided Harris' eyes.

"'Ere, what's the matter with you, Frank?" Harris' solicitude was met by a wall of silence. Harris, disappointed in his failure to appeal to maturity, turned to the lad again. "Well, Johnny boy, looks as though our Frank's dreaming again, thinking about that bird in America . . ."

Ellice sniggered. They had all seen the photographs.

"She's my wife," said Davis quietly, but Harris ignored the interruption to his own train of thought.

"What d'*you* do for it then, Frank? I mean if she's over there and it's true love," he rolled his eyes at Ellice who sniggered again, "what d'you do for nookie?"

"Yeah, Frank what d'you do then?" asked Ellice eagerly, wondering if the answer might not solve his own overwhelming problem of total ignorance in a certain area.

Davis looked at his two persecutors with contempt. "Go without."

"No!" Harris did not believe him and made a violently suggestive gesture which Ellice understood. Davis ignored them.

"You'll grow a bloody hump on your back, mate," said Harris knowledgeably.

"That's preferable to a dose," snapped Davis, while Ellice who had embraced Harris' attitude to women in theory if not in practice, paled at the image Davis' reply conjured up.

"Oh, balls," snapped Harris, "you can't beat a good f . . ."

"If you bastards talked less about fanny and kept your minds on the job we'd all be a lot happier, like." The bosun's voice cut through the chatter like a whiplash. "Paintin' you're supposed to be, not nattering like a bunch of cockle-women on market day, see?"

Harris looked at the retreating figure in the upper 'tween deck. "Fuck off," he mouthed silently and Ellice sniggered again.

Mr Jones continued aft and up the companionway to the upper deck. He picked up a shred of waste that had blown into a corner of the cross alleyway at the head of the ladder and stepped out on deck. Turning aft he walked beneath the port boat davits and ascended the ladder to the helicopter flight deck.

One of the many additions to *Active* during her life, the flat, windswept area had radically altered the ship's appearance. Four men were lowering the safety nets, which stowed vertically at sea, and clearing the deck for the possible arrival of the aircraft.

"When's it due, Bose?"

"Don't know yet."

"Bloody Old Man being cautious again, eh?"

"If you weren't doing this you'd only be sitting in the mess room swilling tea and smoking those filthy cigarettes."

"And thinking about women," added the reproved seaman with a grin, knowing the strong sense of religion the bosun affected in his more saintly moments.

"Dirty bastards," said Theo Jones as he picked another piece of waste out of a scupper and held it up to let the wind carry it leeward.

Naismith looked aft to where Hobden in white boiler suit and yellow, day-glo waistcoat stood and adjusted the ear muffs which depended from his hard-hat.

A few seamen gathered expectantly at the ladder while another in his fire resistant Bristol Fleet suit stood like a yellow samurai at the head of the other ladder, the foam branch at the ready under his arm.

Hobden turned and gave him the thumbs up. The wind and sea had not permitted *Active* to remain at anchor and she steamed slowly north-north-west, half a mile from the wreck. Naismith switched the flight deck indicator lamp to green and turned into the wheelhouse. Bob Sobey, *Active*'s junior deck officer, sat at the Park-Air radio set on 129.7 Mhz.

"What's his ETA now?"

"Seven minutes, sir." Naismith nodded and walked across to the radar. No ships were nearer than eight miles, so he could afford to leave his station by the wreck for a while. The signal caught his eye and he re-read it.

From Captain-Superintendent BNAS
                                   To Master, Active.

Helicopter leaving Plymouth 1000A with diver, will advise buoy requirements later.

He returned to the bridge wing, raised his glasses and swept the horizon. Nothing. Peering again into the radar he saw it on the third sweep. The dot was small and moving towards them rapidly. He spun the bearing cursor and strode to the starboard wing repeater, aligning the azimuth mirror on the same bearing and raising his glasses again.

The sky was clearing, the cold front had passed, the wind chopped round to north-west and the grey scud had been replaced by woolly cumulus and bright blue sky. The waters of the Channel had changed too, to a dark cobalt with white horses glittering and streaking in the sunshine. He saw the aircraft almost at once and picked up his portable handset. "Bridge to flight deck."

"Flight deck to bridge?"

"He's in sight, Chas, and you've got a green light."

"Roger, sir."

He watched Hobden stare to windward and then turn and say something to the men. There was an expectant ripple of movement and Naismith looked up at the blue ensign tugging at the gaff above his head. They could come a point to port without upsetting the pilot. "Steer three-two-five."

"Three-two-five, sir." Still staring at the approaching dot Naismith felt the roll of the ship lessen slightly. It was a question of finding the best compromise. With the wind too broad on the bow the roll would be excessive, although the attitude of the ship would be better for the pilot. With the wind right ahead the rise and fall of the ship would be minimised but the turbulence of the air, and the reduced oxygen content due to the flue gasses from the funnel as it flowed aft over the ship, made the flying trickier.

The blue and silver machine with its grey, whirring disc was coming in fast. The sun glinted off the perspex front as the pilot pulled it into a tight curve to run in head to wind, at a slight angle to *Active*'s course.

"Steady on three-two-five, sir."

"Thank you." There was the difference, Naismith mused. The pilot had covered two miles of sea and was already making his approach before the quartermaster had *Active* steadied on her new course. It was a bit like a marriage, Naismith reflected ironically, an urgent necessary union of otherwise incompatible parts, fraught with dangerous consequences if anything went wrong. He dismissed the thought with bitter self-reproach.

Naismith could see the pilot now as he pulled the nose of the Bolkow 105D up, checking its forward speed and preparing for the last fifty feet of descent. Hobden had signalled the deck's readiness to receive the aircraft with the upraised arms of the semaphore signal "U", ironically that used between ships for standing into danger. The pilot's feet were clearly visible on the pedals and the tail spar of the helicopter twitched, insect-like, in response. Naismith watched in fascinated admiration, his delight in watching almost any activity done well was amply satisfied by the man's skill. Through the perspex he could see the pilot's right hand on the joystick and his left arm disappeared to where Naismith knew it clasped the lever controlling the collective lift. The Bolkow began to assume an apparently stationary position above *Active*'s moving flight deck as the aircraft rose and fell in near-perfect synchronisation with the ship. The roar of its twin gas turbines filled the air and whitened the sea off *Active*'s starboard quarter. Then suddenly the aircraft descended, twitching in line with the ship's centreline at the very moment of touchdown. The pilot gave Naismith a casual wave and out of the aircraft's port door jumped the flight engineer with a bundle of newspapers which he handed to Hobden before opening the passenger door. Two strangers wearing over-large orange survival suits clambered out and moved forward, ducking instinctively from the noisy rotors whirring above their heads. At the rear of the machine the engineer was waving to two of the crew and Hobden motioned for them to move aft. The shell doors were open and Naismith watched them drag out the tanks, lines and pipes that made up the divers' equipment. The engineer came forward and put his mouth to Hobden's ear. There was a pause while another gang of men went aft and dragged a small compressor out of the aircraft's boot and carried it at a weirdly simian lope across the deck, clear of the helicopter. The engineer closed the shell-doors, walked ritually round the aircraft, gave Hobden a thumbs up and clambered in. Naismith could see him belt himself in and fit his headset. Then he heard the Park-Air set crackle and Sobey answer. The next second the aircraft lifted, climbing rapidly and backing slightly. It hovered for a second then the nose came down and it began to speed forwards, coming in low alongside *Active*'s bridge with the aircrew waving and making faces through the perspex.

Naismith jerked a casual and friendly Victory sign at them and grinned as the aircraft banked and climbed into the north-west.

"Hard a starboard."

"Hard a starboard, sir . . ." *Active* turned back

to her monotonous duty of wreck-marking. Aft, the hands were pulling in the nets and securing the deck. Already the samurai had become A.B. Harris again. Not a word had been spoken between Naismith's two helm orders, though the air had been rent by the noise of the helicopter.

Sobey appeared. "Tango Oscar reports he's in contact with Roborough and closes down with us, sir."

"Very good."

Here was Hobden, looming in the port door with a stranger in tow.

"Mr Scranton, sir, senior diver." He stood aside and let the man into the wheelhouse. Naismith held out his hand. "Good morning, Mr Scranton."

"Morning Captain Naismith."

"Have you got all your gear?"

Scranton nodded. "All I need. Is your decompression chamber okay?"

"Not been used since we last put you in it. Coffee?"

"I'll ring for some," put in Hobden, moving to the phone.

Scranton was a middle-aged man, the senior of BNAS's four man diving team. Naismith left him to climb out of the survival suit while he conned *Active* back to her anchorage close to the wreck of the cargo ship *Wallenstein*.

The wind eased as slack water approached and Naismith stood looking down on the boat, slung outboard in the davits, her crew ready and the remaining hands loading the divers' gear. Beside him Susan Paulin, the officer of the watch, was fidgetting.

"What the hell's the matter?" snapped Naismith, suddenly irritable.

"N . . . nothing, sir."

Scranton scrambled into the boat holding his flippers, the scuba gear on his back. He gave Naismith a cheery wave; they had known each other for years. Seeing his boss look up the second diver also looked up at the bridge wing. He was young and he wore no lung so he was clearly going to assist, although all his gear was in the boat ready for him. He wore a Burt Reynolds moustache and, catching sight of Susan Paulin gave an exaggerated wink.

Naismith raised an eyebrow and looked at his second officer.

"Friend of yours?" he asked drily.

"No way," she said colouring slightly.

"He's pretty young to be diving for BNAS," observed Naismith. "I'd have thought a young man with his machismo would have been chasing the big money in the North Sea."

"I think you'll find," said Susan icily, "that he was dismissed from there."

Naismith watched the girl disappear into the wheelhouse. "Now that *was* a piece of feminine behaviour," he muttered to himself. He imagined Walker, the young diver, must have made a pass at the girl. The reflection annoyed him for two reasons. He did not like visitors boarding the ship and behaving as though it was their own private yacht, neither did he like behaviour that was directly attributable to Susan's sex. It reinforced a prejudice he thought he had successfully overcome.

Third Officer Robert Sobey stood in the midships well of the motor boat and watched the divers kit-up. After Scranton was satisfied he lowered his mask and sat, back outboard, on the gunwhale. Giving a thumb's up to Walker he rolled overboard and disappeared with a splash. Walker abstractedly tended Scranton's lifeline and chatted to the boat's crew. Aft the coxswain stood by the tiller and engine control, puffing at a cigarette while the bowman and middle-man had made themselves comfortable and awaited events.

They had left *Active* just before slack water and managed to pick up the floating ends of three of the mooring ropes from the *Wallenstein*.

Walker felt the lifeline jerk. "Okay," he said in an affected mid-Atlantic draw, "you can haul in those ropes. The Chief has just cut them loose."

The boat's crew began hauling in the heavy lines. It took them some time, after which they settled down to wait for Scranton to surface. "He'll be having a look round," explained Walker, "and coming up slowly."

They all knew about the bends and the decompression chamber that was fitted in *Active* against a diving emergency, even though the divers themselves only occasionally worked from the ship. Sobey nodded. Walker was obviously full of bullshit but Sobey was quite content to let him show off unchecked.

"Nitrogen narcosis is a pretty nasty thing you know, and the Chief's getting a bit old for the job . . ."

Sobey did not listen but consulted his watch. He too had done this sort of thing before and knew Scranton had not many more minutes of air left.

Scranton's trail of bubbles appeared close to the boat and a minute later the masked head broke surface. He was wearing, bandolier style, a lifebuoy from the wreck. He ducked out of this and passed it up to the hands reaching out to assist him. It bore the legend: *Wallenstein, Monrovia*. From its frayed line it was clear it had become fouled and failed to float clear when the ship sank.

They dragged the gleaming black figure into the well of the boat with some difficulty. Scranton was ashen-faced beneath his mask. For several minutes he lay panting in the bottom of the boat. Then he wiped his hand across his mouth and muttered, "Tide's turned now, let's get back to the ship . . ."

Naismith picked up the red telephone of the Satellite Communication Saturn Terminal. "*Active*, Master speaking . . ." He listened to his own voice in the earpiece as it made its long journey into space and back again. It always filled him with a sense of wonder, almost childish in its intensity.

"Hullo, James?" He recognised the voice of Douglas Campbell, Captain-Superintendent of BNAS.

"Hullo, sir, all attention."

"I don't want you to bother with that diver, James. Just lay an east cardinal buoy half a cable east of the wreck and come away from the damned thing."

The diver's away now, sir," Naismith frowned, irritated by this shoreside interference with the job. "There are still mooring ropes trailing up from the wreck and although I'm reasonably confident that once they are removed there's no danger to navigation, I have not yet been able to chain-sweep the wreck with the ship."

"Okay, James." Naismith could detect the conciliatory tone of the superintendent overlying the faint exasperation of a senior dealing with a rebellious junior. "It doesn't matter. I just want the buoy laid and you out of it . . ."

"What the hell for?"

"Look James, don't bloody argue." Campbell was angry now and so was Naismith. He had had one job frustrated by a wild goose chase down Channel, his ship's company had been frigged about enough. Campbell must have sensed this for he cooled again. "I understand your sentiments, James, but the matter's . . . sensitive. Leave the job after you've got a buoy on it. Try and get that done before nightfall. Just signal me when it's done. Understand?" Naismith sighed. "Very well. I understand."

"Good. Then, before you come east again I want you to rendezvous the chopper and fill up the Buccabu lighthouse. I'll give you rendezvous details as soon as you let me know that east cardinal buoy's on station. Got it?"

"Roger."

"Best of luck then."

"Thanks."

"Out."

Naismith put the phone down as Hobden put his head into the radio room. "Boat's on its way back, sir."

"Well that saves me another bloody job," said Naismith savagely. "Give the lads a smoke-o then let's get a buoy on this bloody wreck."

Naismith watched the needles of the decometers twitch and move slightly. It invoked another image of childhood: watching the hands of a clock to see the passage of time. They never did until you looked away. Then they seemed to leap suddenly, spanning the seconds of distraction.

Across the wheelhouse Paulin sang out the distance from the wreck in metres.

"Eighty-five, still increasing . . ."

Naismith looked again at the decometers. Like the childhood clock the change was abrupt. He walked briskly across the wheelhouse and leaned over the bridge wing. "Stand by!" The hands looked up at his bellow.

The big yellow and black buoy, paint still tacky and its light winking three rapid flashes of white every five seconds, hung from the derrick, its base just grounded on the deck. Running from the port spurling pipe in the foredeck the buoy chain snaked on deck and wound round the gipsy of the centre capstan and outboard, over the rolled section of *Active*'s port side and vertically downwards to where, thirty metres below, the three-ton cast-iron sinker hung, a little above the bottom.

They were headed west, into the flood tide and the sea. The ship's bow, at dead slow speed rose and fell about six feet, cushioning the effect of the oncoming waves with her flare.

From the sonar Susan Paulin's voice called, "One hundred and ten metres, opening a little to starboard . . ."

"Two-eight-five!" Naismith snapped, stopping the starboard engine. He heard the quartermaster repeat the order and the hard metallic pings of the sonar.

"One hundred and five metres."

"Walk out!" The bosun's arms twitched on the capstan control and Naismith pulled both engine controllers to half astern. Like Hobden he watched the thumping progress of the loaded chain across the deck and over the side, watching for that slight lessening of tension that announced the arrival of the sinker on the seabed.

He saw it at the same moment as Hobden who yelled out "On the botto-o-m! He turned and snapped "Fix!" over his shoulder. Susan called out the sonar range before skipping across to the chart table to read the decometers.

"One hundred, spot on sir!" Naismith watched the chain as Jones continued to pay out the slack. An alarm rang from the chain hold. Its inner end was lifting off the tank tops. One less of those elongated heaps of chain that, tagged with coloured plywood, had lain ready in *Active*'s hold.

He watched for the ship to pull out the slack. He must neither run over the sinker by going ahead, nor drag it closer to the wreck. Ideally he should be stopped over the ground, just moving ahead to counteract the flow of the tide. He stopped the engines and waited, both hands on the engine controllers.

Hobden, still in his white boiler suit which by now was smeared with rusty marks and speckles of yellow gloss, leaned over the side. "Leading a-ahead!"

Naismith gave the engines a short burst at slow ahead.

"E-e-easing." He stopped the engines and walked across to the chart table.

Susan had inked in a dotted circle for the wreck and, almost alongside it to the east, the conventional sign for a cardinal buoy.

"I haven't marked the wreck itself, sir," she said explanatorily. "I didn't think I'd muck the chart up with a dangerous wreck sign and then have to correct it once we'd swept it with a least-depth."

"Very provident of you, Susan," said Naismith approvingly, forgetting the earlier irritation the second officer had caused. They both heard Hobden's cry from the foredeck: "Brought up to the sinker, sir!"

Active was anchored to the buoy mooring. She might yet drag it but already the thumps and clinks from the foredeck told where the hands had the inner end of the chain stopped off on deck with the Blake stopper and the carpenter was shackling it to the bridle of the buoy. The two officers peered into the sonar. Naismith grunted with satisfaction.

"When d'you think we'll sweep the wreck, sir?"

Naismith shrugged. "Don't know."

"It's, er, a bit unusual, isn't it . . . I mean leaving it like this." Susan's tone seemed to suggest an interest that was compounded of apology.

"Bloody irregular. Superintendent said it was 'sensitive'."

Naismith shrugged again. In the irritation he had felt for Campbell and his eagerness to get the buoy laid before the onset of darkness and the freshening of wind he already detected, he had given the matter no thought at all. An order was an order. "Ours but to do and die," he said, turning his attention forward where the buoy had suddenly risen on the derrick purchase and was slewing over the side.

Hobden was looking expectantly up at him as the buoy swung inwards, pendulum-like threatening to thump hard on the ship's side. A seaman deftly swung a fender over and the buoy landed on it, continuing to descend slowly as Naismith nodded his permission to the mate.

"Hard a-starboard."

The helm went over and *Active*, steering in the tide, began a slow turn. A hiss came from alongside as the sea drove the air out of the apron and the buoy suddenly rose on a wave crest. The men straining at the hook lines disengaged the two hooks and Hobden waved the purchase up, clear of the buoy that now bobbed alarmingly alongside, its round shape disturbing the tidal flow down the ship's side more than the entire hull of the *Active*. The bight of the bridle came up on deck to the end of the chain and the stopper. The buoy leaned a little and thumped the side. It was prevented from rushing astern and straightening the bight of chain by a loop of rope at whose ends a seaman waited expectantly. Naismith looked for the buoy chain. It led forward and off the bow at a slowly increasing angle away from it. "Slip the towing line!"

The seaman loosed the rope and hauled in its dripping slackness. The buoy surged aft and the bridle took its weight, leaning it drunkenly as Naismith bellowed "Slip!"

Hobden whirled the maul and brought it unerringly down on the slip of the stopper. The huge tongue lashed savagely and released the chain with a satisfying splash. The buoy jerked vertical and surged away from *Active*'s side as Naismith ordered the helm steadied and rang full-ahead.

"All alight!" sung out Hobden as the men squared-up the foredeck. Beside Naismith Susan checked the lantern with a stopwatch. "Okay?"

"Perfect, sir."

"That's that, then."

Naismith steadied the ship on a course for the Buccabu lighthouse and rang full speed away on the control panel. As the answering buzz from the engine room died away he recollected Susan's unanswered question.

"I suppose," he emphasised the verb cautiously, "it's because the wreck is not technically in the Channel. I daresay some high-powered gentlemen are arguing whose responsibility it is."

Susan Paulin frowned. "But we've put a buoy on it, sir. I mean if it was a matter for a decision about responsibility wouldn't it have been better to wait until after we'd cleared the ropes? You'd as good as told them it wouldn't be dangerous then. Then it'd have been nobody's responsibility."

Susan's logic immediately reproached Naismith for his hasty and ill-considered answer. It was irritating to be reminded of the obvious. He opened his mouth to reproach her but she continued, "You don't think it's anything to do with that submarine, do you sir?"

Submarine? Naismith had forgotten about the submarine. He had viewed the sonar echo with a somewhat jaundiced eye in the early hours. A ship's master gets a variety of calls to the bridge in the small hours. The quality for which he is called at such moments, his experience, is often a subconscious arbiter as to the immediacy of the danger his subordinate considers important enough to rouse him, for Susan's submarine had not rated very highly on his list of imminent dangers. After all he was only thirty-eight. Submarines were things he knew little about. Naismith hadn't even had the benefit of Quartermaster Potts's naval war games. He did not think Campbell's order had anything at all to do with the submarine. If it was a bloody submarine.

"No I don't!" He said sharply. He took one look round the horizon and stumped off the bridge.

The unexpected knock on his cabin door only further exacerbated the annoyance Naismith already felt for the outcome of the *Wallenstein* business. A cautious but thorough man, he liked also to do a job well, to complete it. It was his own brand of signature on his own artistry. He resented the intrusion of even his superiors.

"Yes? What is it?"

"'S me, captain, can I have a word?" Scranton,

in the divers' undress uniform of singlet, jeans and heavily armoured wristwatch lurched into the cabin. He held out a half-empty whisky bottle. "Care for a drink?"

This piece of effrontery silenced Naismith for long enough to enable Scranton to seat himself on the cabin settee. It occurred to Naismith that he had not had time to debrief the diver, and was in part guilty of discourtesy. Although he strongly disapproved of Scranton's obvious intoxication he indulged himself to the extent of submitting to a sudden desire to share the spirit. He reached for a pair of glasses and set them on the coffee table that sat in the centre of his cabin, a concession to his dignity as master.

"Thank you." He tried to gauge how drunk Scranton was and concluded not very, but that it was probably an habitual condition. He made allowances for an old acquaintance and reflected that there had never been any doubts about Scranton's professional abilities.

"Sorry I didn't have a chance to speak to you before laying that buoy. Bit of a paddy on to get it done." Scranton nodded and poured the whisky without a tremor. "Cheers."

"Cheers." Scranton shrugged. "Hadn't finished the job, captain; any reason for not finishing the job?"

"Not really. Only that I was told to leave it as it was." Naismith's mood improved as soon as the whisky hit his stomach.

"Nothing to do with me?" asked Scranton, narrowing his eyes.

"Not as far as I know . . . why d'you ask?"

Scranton shrugged, stared at Naismith, then down at the carpet. As soon as he began to speak Naismith knew he was drunk.

"I'm getting a bit long in the tooth for this kind of thing, Captain." He swallowed a big slug and slopped another large shot into the glass. "I only just got through my last medical you know . . ."

"You should be careful then . . ." Naismith indicated the whisky.

"It's just a fucking regulation . . . bloody world's stiff with fucking regulations. You won't be able to fart soon without breaking the bloody law. Christ, I'm a man, not a sodding machine . . ."

A horrible vision of himself appearing at an inquest occurred to Naismith. What if something had happened to Scranton? He sipped the whisky and cursed his imagination. Keep the conversation professional, he told himself.

"What did you find down there this afternoon?"

"Eh?" Scranton's head came up. His eyes were already bleary and he frowned. He had clearly drunk his whisky fast. Or was very used to it and reacted quickly. But he made an effort to recover himself. "You saw the life belt?"

Naismith nodded.

"It's the *Wallenstein* all right. Three hatches, accommodation aft, built Howaldtswerke Hamburg, 1968. Read it on the bridge front, sold to Liberian interests I s'pose . . ." He seemed pleased with that information as though it demonstrated his competence, fulfilling Naismith's first task, a positive identification of the wreck. "All the mooring ropes were trailing up from the stern. We got three cut away before the tide turned but there are two more."

"Two?"

"Uh huh," Scranton nodded, "big 'uns."

Naismith bit his lip in annoyance. They had so nearly completed the job. But slack water had lasted nearly half an hour. "What else did you notice?"

A curiously pained look crossed Scranton's face. "She went down on her port side, about a twenty-degree list. Bloody great gash along her side, opened up both number two hold and number three. Bulwarks all ripped and some of the deck cargo of drums stowed on the port side of the deck had dropped through onto the seabed. There was another hole aft, into her engine room. Much smaller and above the water line. Looked like the colliding ship had had two goes and as she listed it allowed water into the engine room. The main gash looked like anchor damage, the other vessel's anchor may have caught. I've known it happen before."

"Yes, yes, go on. Anything else?"

"Two dust carts on the starboard side. All painted up with 'City of Santa Maria de los Mayas' in Spanish on the side."

"Visibility was good then?"

Scranton seemed to think there was a doubt about the information he was giving Naismith. "Look Captain, I'm a bloody good diver. I notice things, details. That's the information you wanted, isn't it?" Again that pained, insulted look.

"Yes, of course. I'm just surprised you could see so well at that depth."

"Well I could see bloody well. I used a flashlight and you have to swim close to things, very close but I noticed those details . . . I noticed them all right."

"Any, er . . ."

"Bodies?"

Naismith nodded.

"Not that *I* was going to recover." Scranton slammed the glass down on the coffee table and put his face in his hands. "You see them at the ports," he mumbled through his fingers, "A man in an upper deck cabin that could have been the radio room . . ." That would account for one of the missing men, Naismith thought, avoiding the horrifying image in his mind's eye. "And when I went to read the builder's plate I saw another. Cabin under the bridge, the old man's I suppose . . . woman's face, 'bout thirty-five, fair hair, all floating about like fucking seaweed . . ." Naismith got up and patted him on the shoulder. The tears were streaming down Scranton's cheeks, leaking between the powerful fingers in an attempt to hide his weakness behind his remaining physical assets.

"I'm going up to the bridge, Scranton," he said quietly. "I should get turned in now."

When he returned fifteen minutes later Scranton and the whisky had gone.

Chapter Five

Naismith turned forward, ordered an adjustment of course and rang the engines to full-ahead to regain station. The Bolkow roared away over the sea, the big neoprene bag containing diesel oil hanging below it like the corpse of a shiny black pig. It was the fifth to be air-lifted across to the Buccabu lighthouse and Naismith transferred his attention to the slender granite tower half a mile away to the south-west.

It was a fresh, blue-water morning. The force-six wind tumbled the sea in a riot of foaming crests between which the sabre-winged fulmars glided on their constant patrol for food. There had been a slight delay in hooking up that last load and *Active* had got too far to the east, pushed by wind and tide away from the lighthouse.

Through the binoculars Naismith could see the keepers on the flat platform built above the light, the twentieth-century gimmicky structure added to the massive granite Victorian tower, the grace of its tapering shape belying the enormity of its mass. The swells burst at its base, swirling over the jutting plinth of the old landing and exploding in bursts of pure white halfway up the structure itself. He remembered the patient days, sometimes weeks, of waiting to relieve the keepers by boat; of the ice-slippery set-off with its film of treacherous weed from which more than one keeper had been swept into the sea. And he remembered the keepers themselves, slung from the derrick as it slewed round to lower them into the boat which snapped at its head and sternlines in the foaming maelstrom that surged, sucked and gurgled round the solitary rock even on a 'calm' day. They were whey-faced and weak, those men, from two months incarceration in that forbidding prison, while their reliefs, coming off from the delights of the shore, were whey-faced and weak from the hangover their last night ashore had induced.

But that was all history now. Naismith had been Third Officer then, spent most of his waking hours in the boats, his hands as horny as any seaman's, his face browned from exposure. That had all been before the arrival of the helicopter, he mused, watching the Bolkow shed its load from the magnetic slip and head back to *Active*. He adjusted the ship's head again and slowed the engines, lifting his glasses to watch a gannet chased by a great skua. The beautiful solan goose tried to evade the big, dark predator but in the end the skua won. The gannet regurgitated its food and the skua twisted in hot pursuit to eat it.

"Tango Oscar requests permission to land on and fuel after the next oil bag, and the lighthouse reports the helipad will be congested after the next load, sir."

Naismith nodded at Sobey, who returned to the radio. Six bags of oil had followed four of water and it would take some time to run that quantity down the tower and into the storage tanks. He picked up his handset.

"Bridge – aft"

"Aft – bridge?" Hobden's voice came through.

"Tango Oscar landing on to fuel after the next load.

I'll tell him to shut down and you can lash him. The keepers will be some time clearing the helipad so you can stand the lads down for a while . . ."

"Aye, aye. Fuel and shut down, over."

"Out."

The blue and silver Bolkow was already banking and making her approach. Hobden gave him the visual signal to hook-up while in the middle of the flight deck one of the seamen, hard-hatted, earmuffed and gaudily waistcoated, held the sling up and waited for the aircraft.

The door of the Bolkow opened and the engineer's head appeared. He was on his hands and knees, talking the pilot down. The Bolkow made its descent, a vector of almost mathematical precision with *Active*'s pitch. Naismith felt the hairs cawling on his neck in admiration and excitement and dread of anything going fearfully wrong and dumping that screaming, whirling mass of potent machinery on his defenceless ship. His vivid imagination did not think that Samurai Harris and his foam branch would achieve a great deal against the fireball that training films had led him to expect.

Beneath the silver belly of the helicopter hung the four-legged lifting sling. The hook-up man grabbed the bolt trigger with one hand and automatically crouched and stood up as the Bolkow squatted over him, the pilot continually adjusting his height above the deck. The hook-up man inserted the eye of the strop into the magnetic slip and triggered the bolt, running clear of the aircraft's skids with both thumbs up. The Bolkow began to climb vertically. Naismith saw it jerk as it took the weight, *Active* dipping her stern and depriving the heavy oil bag of support at precisely the same moment. Then the chopper was swinging away, nose down and accelerating for the lighthouse.

Naismith passed instructions to the pilot via Sobey and heard them acknowledged. Then he walked across the wheelhouse and ordered coffee.

They made quite a social gathering in the wheelhouse ten minutes later. The quartermaster still stood at the wheel and Naismith still had the con, glancing out of the wheelhouse windows as *Active* stemmed the tide at dead slow. But there was no shipping close-to, only a group of coasters rounding the point to the north-west and some deep-water ships three miles to the southward. Hobden was there, relaxing with coffee and chatting to the flight engineer in his smart blue flying suit; Sobey had emerged from the radio room and Susan had appeared, her eyes still heavy from sleep. Next to Naismith the pilot looked forward at the buoys on the foredeck, staring at the other man's professional hardware with intelligent interest.

"How goes it then, James?"

"Not too bad, Greg . . ." He took the proffered telex and read it. It was the pilot's instructions, originating from Campbell. The last sentence brought Naismith's head up frowning. "You've got to take the divers off?"

"That's what it says."

"But they haven't finished clearing the wreck . . ." He tailed off, aware that the matter was of no interest to the pilot. He tried to remember what he had said to Campbell. He remembered telling him that the diver was already at work. Had Campbell construed that the clearing operation had been completed? Did he want the diver removed on that assumption, or was he adamant that Naismith, having laid the buoy, had completed the work expected of him?

"Excuse me . . ." He went into the radio room and checked the signal file for the acknowledgement to his last message, sent after the embarrassing interview with Scranton. It had informed the powers-that-be that an east cardinal buoy had been laid on the wreck, one hundred metres east of the *Wallenstein*, and that *Active* was on passage to the Buccabu Rock lighthouse to arrive at daylight.

He flicked over to the next green sheet. *Your 21/1930z acknowledged. Helicopter rendezvous arranged for Buccabu at 22/0930z.*

No mention of divers.

Naismith picked up the red handset of the Satellite Communications system and punched in the digits for the Goonhilly aerial. He heard the tone change and picked off the Auto numerals, the U.K. code and then the PSTN number. Twenty seconds later he heard Campbell's voice.

"Superintendent?"

"Morning sir, Naismith here."

"Hullo James, how goes it?"

"At the Buccabu light how, about halfway through. Reckon to be away about fifteen hundred. D'you want me to get rid of this diver or go back to the wreck and finish the job?"

"No James, leave the wreck for the time being. Discharge the diver and then anchor in Falmouth. I don't want you returning east until I've cleared up one or two things. Understand?"

Naismith was still somewhat in the dark, though the immediate dilemma was solved.

"More or less, sir."

"Good. I'll give you further orders by signal later."

Campbell paused and then added by way of partial explanation, "It's still a bit sensitive, James. You wait in Falmouth until you hear from me."

"Aye, aye, sir." Naismith put down the phone, failing to note the incongruity of the ancient acknowledgement in its archaic form winging its way into space and back to Campbell's desk.

He returned to the wheelhouse to finish his coffee. In the chart room Sobey sorted through the mail passed to him by the flight engineer.

The helicopter roared out on the beam with the last bag of fresh water, 360 litres of it. When it had been drained into the lighthouse's tanks the station would be filled. With winter coming on Naismith felt justifiably pleased. He called into the wheelhouse to Sobey.

"Let the divers know that in about half an hour the chopper will be ready to take them off."

"Aye, aye, sir."

Naismith turned back to watch the helicopter as it banked to approach the top of the tower.

"Bloody hell!" He watched the jettisoned bag hurtle through the air and hit the water with a splash. He picked up the portable VHF.

"Bridge – Aft!"

"Aft – Bridge, I see it, sir. Over."

"Get the crash boat away, Chas, and recover that bag!"

He saw Hobden wave acknowledgement and turned to the quartermaster.

"Hard a port!" *Active* turned to give the boat a lee as Sobey came out of the radio room.

"Tango Oscar reports engine trouble, sir."

"Does he want to land?"

"No sir, he says he'll make direct for Penzance. He's gaining height and asks us to monitor him until he touches down."

"Right." Naismith looked at the helicopter which had climbed until it was a silver speck in the sky and already heading for the blue line of the Cornish coast. He guessed one engine had packed up and snapped at the third officer, "Jump in the boat, Mr Sobey, and go and get that bloody pillow tank. Tow it alongside, don't try and empty it, we don't want salt water in it . . ."

"Aye, aye, sir."

Naismith steadied *Active* and waited a moment while Sobey got himself down to the boat deck.

"Lower away!" He watched the boat descend and hit the water with a smack. A few seconds later it swung away from the ship's side in pursuit of the neoprene pillow tank. It was only then that it occurred to Naismith that the helicopter's abrupt departure meant that the divers would be left on board *Active*.

Seaman Davis was tired. He was aware of having worked hard during the helicopter operation, earning, he hoped, the approval of the impassive Mr Hobden. He did not like Hobden but after the ear-splitting clatter and excitement of the day he had learned respect. It was a respect that extended also to his new shipmates. His physical exhaustion was pleasurable as he relaxed in the camaraderie of the mess deck. Bosun Jones had seemed pleased too, and had said "Well done!"

He was aware of a subtle change in the atmosphere and turned to find Second Officer Paulin had come into the mess. She had a handful of letters which she distributed. One of them was for Frank Davis and it bore a Central American stamp. She gave him a smile as he took it. He touched the medallion that gleamed on his breast and felt his heartbeat quicken. It seemed that a higher authority than even Captain Naismith himself approved of his conduct that day. He slipped into his cabin to read the letter.

Three hours later *Active* dropped her anchor in Carrick Roads and Mr Hobden announced there would be a run ashore for off-duty personnel in Falmouth. By closing time, as *Active*'s off-duty watch reeled its merry way back to the harbour steps and the waiting boat, Davis was roaring drunk.

Chapter Six

Naismith woke in anticipation of a good day. He had slept well and peered eastward en route to his shower to see the sun peeping over the tree line of the Roseland peninsula, adding a dull lustre to the sombre battlements of St Mawes Castle. He imagined that they would shortly receive a message to return east and leave the wreck of the *Wallenstein* with its single buoy. Whatever the nature of the "sensitivity" over the wreck it was clear it did not concern him and, like a good subordinate, he could forget the matter. A pleasant day running up the Channel would give him a chance to catch up on his paperwork and perhaps allow him an hour or two of leisure to go and occupy the carpenter's shop and finish the half model of *Active*'s hull he had started months ago.

He emerged from the shower and shaved, whistling quietly to himself. After the petty aggravations of the last two days he enjoyed the compensation of being his own boss, of savouring the pleasure of command. He knew it to be a rare privilege with moments of even rarer relaxation like the present one.

A deck below and already dressed Charles Hobden sat, his face a mask, and listened to Bosun Jones.

"Can't hide it, like. Bloody man's too drunk to get out of bed . . . I don't mind the boys having a few as long as they goes to bed quiet, like . . ."

"Did he go to bed quietly?" Hobden interrupted. There was a pause as Theo Jones, mindful of the strictures of testament upon the matter, considered his reply.

"He didn't make what you'd call 'a noise', sir." Hobden sighed with comprehension.

"You mean he made a mess, then."

Jones nodded. "Threw up everywhere . . ." Hobden stood up and led the way below.

The smell of vomit filled the alleyway and Hobden's nose wrinkled in disgust. He threw open the cabin door. Still dressed in jeans and socks, Davis lay upon a soiled bunk. He had wet himself.

His face had the relaxed look of a baby about it, an impression heightened by the empty bottle of rum that he clutched. A sheen of unhealthy sweat lay on his pallid forehead and the stubble of his beard was blue against his cheek.

"Bombed out," offered his cabin mate who was diligently making his own bunk.

Hobden gave the lad a jaundiced look. He leaned over Davis and pressed gently with one finger on the side of Davis's head, just in front of his ear. Davis stirred but did not wake.

"Get this lot cleaned up and disinfected. Leave the bedding until he comes to." Hobden indicated the pool of vomit on the deck and down the side of the drawers. "I want to know the minute he comes to. Got it?"

Davis' cabin mate nodded unhappily.

Hobden ruined Naismith's day just as the captain called for his second cup of coffee. He did not impart the full details in front of the whole saloon, just intimated there was trouble.

"One of the men incapable of turning out this morning, sir. Can I see you about it after breakfast?"

Naismith nodded. "Okay. Drunk?" Hobden nodded and attacked the grapefruit without enthusiasm.

It was eleven o'clock in the morning when Davis woke. It was almost twelve by the time his mates had got him into a fit state to be hauled before the captain. Naismith did not enjoy disciplinary matters. He and Hobden, Chief Engineer Morrison and Mr Jones agreed that a firm discipline ought to prevent the kind of outbreak of behaviour now under consideration. Naismith looked up at the defaulter, at Hobden and Jones, witnesses to the affair in hand.

Naismith forsook the cautious, official peroration designed to avoid giving grounds for misinterpretation, conceived by pettifogging and impractical practitioners of industrial law. There was no doubt of Davis' guilt.

"What have you to say to justify your behaviour, Davis?"

There was an incoherent mumble from the top of Davis's head. Drunken contrition was a condition that roused only further irritation in the aggravated breast of James Naismith. His perfect day had been ruined, the morning largely taken up by listening to the reports on Davis' conduct. He forced himself to be patient.

"Pay attention Davis. You have committed a dismissable offence, not by getting drunk last night but by failing to turn out this morning *due* to being drunk last night. A drunken idiot on the deck of this ship could cause a serious accident. In view of what you asked me the other day I regard this misconduct very seriously and I require an explanation."

Davis lifted his face. It was less than an hour since

he had woken from his stupor to face this day. This terrible, terrible day. In the priorities of his mind as it awoke to consciousness came first the agony of excess. The hangover was massive, but as he accepted it he sought its reason, aware that it hung, lurking in the shadows of his suffering brain. And then it came to him, in a rush, rebuking him for forgetting in his own weakness, even for a single second.

Death. Death. Death. Death. It beat in his head with the throb of his pain. *Muerte. Muerte.*

Carlos Miguel was dead. The son he had never seen. Would never see. He felt the waves of anger that spewed from him in the renewed contractions of his guts. But they heaved on void. Nothing. Emptiness.

Death.

Naismith's face swam towards him. He could not grasp what he had done, could not see it from the captain's point of view. Naismith and his ship, his attitudes, way of life, of all their bloody lives here in this stuffy cabin with the brass fittings and the ridiculous chintz upholstery, mocked him with its smug Englishness.

His face contracted and Naismith was suddenly reminded of a crucifixion, guessing the reason in some intuitive way before the words of explanation came slowly from Davis.

"My son is dead."

Naismith remembered the letter with the exotic stamp and the tricoloured border. He remembered the two photographs Davis carried. "Take him below and let him turn in. Someone is to keep an eye on him, Bose. I mean that very seriously . . ." Neither Jones nor Hobden quite understood.

"He might try and do something foolish." He looked at the seaman. "All right Davis," said Naismith as the tears began to stream down the man's face, "go below now."

It was only in the silence that filled the cabin after they had helped Davis away, that Naismith considered the strange coincidence of two men weeping in his cabin within two days.

Sobey knocked on the captain's cabin door ten minutes later. "Beg pardon, sir, but this signal's just come in on the telex." He handed Naismith the chit. After the preamble and address Naismith read: *Remove east cardinal buoy from wreck of* Wallenstein *and resume work in Dover Strait.*

"Shit!" he said. It did not make sense. The remaining ropes still constituted a danger. That was why the wreck had been marked. Why should they now remove the buoy?

Dawn the following morning found *Active* ten miles to the north-west of the position of the wreck. She had steamed at reduced speed overnight to reach her task at daylight. At 0600 Hobden called Naismith who answered the telephone and then stretched in his bunk and let the events of the previous day wash over him in sad reflection. They had not left Falmouth until late afternoon, Hobden taking the opportunity of the unusual idleness to scrub and touch up the ship's water line. After they had sailed Naismith had gone down into Davis's cabin and sat with him. Little by little the contents of the letter had come out.

Naismith could see it was a very long letter in Spanish. It was smudged and stained by tears, though whether those of the writer, the reader, or both, he did not know. Since it contained much more than the information of the death of Juanita's baby, Naismith got the impression that Davis was only just assimilating parts of it, parts that he had not read earlier after learning that first, dreadful news.

Then it occurred to Naismith that it was in fact two letters. The first long, written like a diary, an attempt by Juanita to share the increasing horror of her days with her distant husband. The second and final page contained the personal tragedy.

Naismith only understood imperfectly, trying patiently to unravel the sobbing sentences Davis seemed to want to share. As he listened, Naismith became aware that Davis' first shock of grief was passing with his hangover. It was being replaced by a dry-eyed and feverish anger. Remembering the BBC documentary about Costa Maya, Naismith felt a bitter helplessness rising in himself. An unpolitical animal with the contempt many seamen feel for place-seeking and self-interested politicians, Juanita's story seemed appalling in the enormity of its outrage. Despite the disjointed recital of events that Davis gave him, Naismith's imagination evoked the essential horrors of a month of terror in the far-off and sun drenched "paradise".

The peasant rising against the military government had spread like a bush fire. Arms had appeared bearing Czechoslovakian, Russian and Chinese markings. The well-disciplined and single-minded cadres of hard-core Communists had shown a military competence far superior to the bumbling efforts of the jünta's staff. Government successes, though loudly trumpeted in the newspapers and diffused abroad, particularly in the United States, had scarcely any real military effect upon the war. The bloody reprisals against villages suspected of sheltering guerillas were common enough, familiar to a world used to accepting such things on its television screens. They only served to increase the implacable collective will of the peasantry, so that the sympathy of the countryside swiftly favoured the anti-government forces. Where government troops scored notable successes against armed resistance, it was usually in the rooting out of badly organised guerrilla groups. Men and women who died gun in hand held together by bonds of passionate conviction rather than military sense, gave the army a false sense of initial superiority. It was not long before these spontaneous little bands had been destroyed, betrayed or melted away to join the better-organised Communist-led militia in the interior.

It was only a matter of months before the towns and larger villages of the country were heavily garrisoned. Their populations, of divided sympathies and largely undeclared loyalties, were under curfew and attempting to lead normal lives in spite of little intercourse with the food-producing countryside and a constant military presence. At first the insurgents retired to train and equip in the mountains and jungles. A sense of quiet had fallen over the land, of illusory government success. Western neighbours were assured stability had been restored. Journalists and travellers told a different tale, of a land expectant of renewed violence.

At first it was hardly noticeable; a few desultory attacks on the most remote garrisons, the severing of supply lines. All the age-old responses of irregular warfare: hit and run. Then came intimation of a more serious and better coordinated operation. A series of mysterious explosions destroyed the American built gun-ships as they lay on the concrete helipads of their heavily guarded airfields. There was even one spectacular mid-air explosion of a helicopter over the very heart of the capital at the hour of *paseo*.

The offensive built up with terrifying speed; the army, half-believing its own propaganda, was caught at a disadvantage. Its garrisons were besieged, cut off by a half-trained corps of women, youths and old men to whom the Kalashnikov had the potency of the now discarded rosary. There were brilliant exceptions. Sorties and courageous stands of young army officers who died cursing their incompetent superiors. They died in the bitter knowledge that their lives had been ended by old men, children and women. But their heroism had no effect upon the tide of events. The fit males were elsewhere. Soon gunfire was heard in the streets of Santa Maria and a week later the fully trained guerilla "brigades" were into the city's outskirts. The dockland suburb of Santa Maria called Santiago fell almost without the inhabitants knowing it. The river divided Santiago from the business centre and government offices, the cathedral and presidential palace of Santa Maria proper. One night the government forces consolidated their position, blew the Jesus and Mary bridge and abandoned the Santiago suburb. It was considered militarily worthless, a flat area of reclaimed marshland that could be commanded by the heavy artillery on the heights of the citadel hill round which the essential heart of Santa Maria beat.

Santiago was a dockland and residential suburb of the working class that faded imperceptibly into shanty townships and finally small fields and plantations. It was pointless to defend it and risk a costly action in house-to-house fighting. The docks were abandoned partly out of panic and partly because the main airfield, now under strong military control, lay on the plateau to the north of the city, on the far side from Santiago. Aid would come swiftly by air, it was argued, and the artillery commanding the south would effectively control the dock wharves and render them no-man's-land for the time being. Besides, at the fashionable resort of the Baia Mayor three miles along the coast, there was an excellent deep water anchorage and the facilities of the naval base of San Nicolo.

So Santiago was abandoned and Juanita and her baby woke to the sight of unfamiliarly armed men prowling the streets. It was some minutes before she realised what had happened but then the joy she felt had led her to leave her baby with her mother and rush into the streets waving a scarlet scarf that Francis had given her. It was pure silk and rippled with the speed of her running, and soon other sympathisers were in the streets, welcoming and feeding their deliverers.

It was then that the shells began to arrive from the citadel.

And one of them killed Carlos Miguel and his grandmother.

Most of this Naismith learned from his long wait with Davis. Some of it, he recollected later, he had half-assimilated from reports on television and in British newspapers. But the burden of it seemed now to linger oppressively. He knew that Davis would not attempt suicide. Naismith could see the burning of deep anger in eyes that fed now upon a desire to live. The purpose of Davis' life from that moment had nothing in common with his own, nor the *Active*. But Naismith had asked the man not to rush off the ship, to stay and work his month on duty.

Davis had come out of his stupor and refocused his eyes on the captain, sitting incongruously in the cabin. Naismith saw the beginning of contemptuous scorn cross Davis' face. He realised with a sickening lurch that Davis probably saw him as a representative of that right-wing reaction that had killed his child.

"You'll have just about enough money to fly the Atlantic," he said quietly. He saw Davis' expression change, first to puzzlement then comprehension. The Atlantic was the barrier. He felt sure that once across the ocean he would find some means of travelling to Santa Maria. A month's wages would provide for that at least.

"I never thought of that," Davis said simply, his opinion of the captain changing.

Later Naismith pondered the matter. He imagined the effect of losing either of his own children. The thought appalled him even as he was aware of the difference between Davis' love for Juanita and his own unsatisfactory relationship with his own wife. The comparison worried him all the remainder of that day, displacing the more horrible prospect of loosing either of his children and reminding him of that curious dilemma of modern man; that with all the advantages civilisation had conferred, he basically remained dissatisfied.

He found he could not sleep and went up on the bridge at one in the morning. He wondered if, had his second officer been male, he would have troubled to get out of his bunk, but he did not seek Susan out. He merely leaned on the rail.

It was a beautiful night. The wind had hauled to the north and blew at force four. A crescent moon drifted in and out of puffs of cumulus and the stars shone with the brilliant sharpness imparted by cold, clear air. The sea lay dark beneath the arch of the sky and Naismith was moved by the sheer perfection of infinity. *Active*, under easy revolutions, lifted with a kind of majesty upon the water, a tiny speck upon its vastness, evidence of man's ingenuity in the hostile environment.

But tonight the enchantment of the night was spoiled by the very presence of the ship he was proud to command. The complacent and romantic images *Active* called to mind were lies. Tonight he felt his ship lay in the ocean like the spirochete of disease.

It was the feeling of self-disgust that sent him in search of Susan. He found her on the opposite bridge wing. She was humming to herself and stopped, surprised to see him.

"Oh! It's a lovely night, sir."

"Mmm." Naismith grunted noncommitally. But Susan's good mood was more durable. "'When I look out on such a night as this, I feel as if there could be neither wickedness nor sorrow in the world . . .'"

"Is that another of your quotations?" Naismith asked.

"Yes. Jane Austen. She went on to say something about people being less wicked if they contemplated nature more . . . I can't remember it exactly . . ." Her voice trailed off. She wanted to ask why he could not sleep but second officers, even curious female ones, did not ask the masters of ships questions like that.

"Yes," said Naismith after a pause, "I suppose she was right, but she could afford to be genteely philosophical. It's too late now . . ." He began to tell her about Davis and his wife and child, about the remote and vicious war in Central America. Susan felt touched by the tale, not only because of the sad death of Davis' son, but because it seemed that there was no hope left in the world. Above them the stars shone impassively, their sparkling fire cold in the infinity of the sky.

"Strange that the *Wallenstein* should have been on passage to the same place," Naismith concluded. "It somehow makes the whole thing real, having a member of the ship's company involved."

"It's a mistake to think we aren't involved. I mean this sort of coincidence just highlights the point I've been trying to make about the world being no more than a global village . . ." she began and Naismith felt no rising exasperation at the prospect of her preaching. Neither did he feel any need to hide behind the barrier of rank. Suddenly the fourteen years difference in their ages disappeared and he was as delighted as she when she pointed and cried out:

"Oh, look!"

They saw the dolphins coming in at an angle on the starboard bow, dark shapes that tore a faint trace of phosphorescence from the sea. More clearly they heard the irregular slaps of their gambolling re-entry as they leapt in line with the ship, splashing in the wash that spread out either side of *Active*'s bow. Ten minutes later they had gone.

"We are going too slow for them," said Naismith, disappointed at their departure.

"It's encouraging to see them, though," said Susan, glad of the change of subject and trying to recall her former happy frame of mind. She remembered the captain's story about the porpoises and dolphins of his childhood. She turned towards him and was going to remind him that they had just observed cetacean life in the waters of the Channel again. But the captain seemed about to speak and his expression, even in the moonlight, did not seem to encourage a reminder of former confidences. And when he did speak he was clearly abstracted and had forgotten she was there.

"I wonder," he said almost wistfully, "why man always has to fuck everything up?"

As he stretched and recalled the previous day's events Naismith threw his legs out of the bunk with the tired realisation that he had not slept enough. His lingering on the bridge until well into the middle watch had been a stupid thing to do. He showered and went on the bridge. Charles Hobden greeted him and lowered the glasses. The silhouettes of several ships were visible on the horizon ahead, merchantmen making down from the Channel lightvessel towards Ushant. Naismith picked up his own binoculars and swept the horizon, more out of habit than any real interest.

"D'you see it, sir?" asked Hobden.

"Eh?" Naismith frowned and concentrated, not wishing to appear to have missed anything of significance. Right ahead of them lay the grey shape of a warship. There was no tell-tale wisp of white at her bow to indicate movement. She was stationary. A faint sensation of unease again crawled along Naismith's spine even as his conscious mind assimilated the intelligence that the warship was some seven miles distant.

"How far to the buoy, Chas?"

"Seven point three miles."

"And our grey-funneled friend?"

"Seven point two-five."

"He's sitting on top of the wreck." Hobden grunted concurrence and both officers stared at the warship.

"Type 42 . . . wonder what the hell she's doing there?"

"Anything to do with what the boss said about it

93

being 'sensitive', d'you think?" volunteered Hobden. Naismith frowned. He could not for the life of him understand the precise nature of the connection but he had a kind of intuitive feeling that Hobden was right. There was something about the wreck of the *Wallenstein* that was very odd.

"I suppose he's got his divers on the wreck," observed Hobden, voicing the thought rising in Naismith's mind.

"Yes, but what for?"

"Gold, sir?" offered Quartermaster Shuter, a normally talkative man to whom duty on the four-to-eight watch with the taciturn mate was an ordeal. "Like the *Edinburgh*?"

Hobden shrugged. "It's possible . . . could be arms or something. She was going out to that place where all the fighting is . . ."

"Well the destroyer's calling us on the aldis, Chas. You'd better answer her."

Chapter Seven

Active's crew stared to starboard with ill-concealed curiosity as, with main derrick swung over, Naismith made his approach to recover the buoy. It was close ahead of the destroyer which lay stopped and head to the ebb tide as *Active* passed her port side. The naval ratings on deck stared back, equally curious. Her diving party were clearly visible, assembled at the top of a jacob's ladder leading down to a grey Zodiac inflatable in which three more gleaming black figures sat watching.

Behind him Naismith heard the slight squeal of the sheave in the gaff block as a seaman dipped the blue BNAS ensign. The knot of watching officers on the destroyer's bridge wing looked up at their own ensign and then one of them ordered a rating to respond. Naismith waved, then turned to concentrate on conning *Active*. He was vaguely aware of the whirr and click of Sobey's motor-driven Nikon, and the hum of the machinery in the lean grey hull.

"It's *Harwich*, sir, the Type 42 that's supposed to have sunk an Argie submarine in the Falklands campaign," said Sobey excitedly, training the Nikon on the fine view of the slender hull as it came end-on to the observers on *Active*.

"A sleek grey messenger of death," said Sobey, still operating the Nikon frantically. Naismith found the young man's callous comment disturbing, then dismissed the destroyer from his mind as he closed the last few metres to the bobbing buoy.

He had *Active* within five degrees of the tide, aware that the westerly breeze would begin to have its effect in slewing the ship if the hands were not fairly nimble. He stopped the engines thrashing astern and watched the buoy's progress down the ship's side slowly reverse. The buoy was some eight feet off. He kicked the port engine ahead and put the helm hard over to starboard and waited. The gyro repeater under his elbow clicked once, twice. They stopped just ahead of *Harwich*.

"Midships!" He stopped the port engine. The buoy lay bereft of relative motion some six feet off the ship's side. A bight of rope, thrown by two men in a practised gesture, snaked out from the ship's side where Hobden had the hands mustered and fell over the diamond shape of the double conical topmark. The buoy leaned to the sudden weight as four men heaved it in to the ship's side.

Naismith kicked both engines dead slow ahead and nodded at Hobden's expectant face. The two life-jacketed seamen scrambled down the jumping ladder and chose their moment. Naismith stopped the engines. Holding the buoy superstructure with one hand and holding out their free hands the two seamen grabbed the heavy wire slings with their big steel hooks. There was a minute of struggle, the buoy bobbed alongside and bumped *Active*'s hull, threatening to throw them off into the tide which sucked past at a knot and a half. As each seaman gave a triumphant yell of success a man on deck pulled the light line attached to the hook's eye. This applied tension to the hook until both had been inserted and the weight could be taken evenly by the main derrick slings.

"Heave up!" Shouted Hobden with a hand signal to the winchman and the heavy purchase wound in, lifting the buoy clear of the sea with a hiss of draining water *Active* leaned to the weight. Level with the deck its elevation was briefly halted while the two men jumped off and divested themselves of their life jackets.

Active was anchored by the derrick head now, and Naismith applied port holm to counteract the wind which was blowing them over the buoy chain. The consequences of leaning on the chain with the weight of the ship while the buoy remained suspended by the derrick head could be serious.

"Sir?" Sorey was fussing at the wheelhouse door. "Message from *Harwich*, sir . . ."

"Not now, for Christ's sake, tell the bugger to stand-by . . ." he snapped. A vision of *Harwich*'s captain, his bridge milling with officers and ratings, wanting to find some means of stamping his personal touch upon the morning's proceedings irritated him. There had been that brief exchange of signals as they had approached in which Naismith had detected more than a little early-morning acid.

Damn it, he thought, he had his orders and they were specific and imperative. He was not engaged in war games and had little taste for them.

He heard Sobey asking the warship to wait.

Hobden had the purchase chock-a-block now and had slewed the derrick head as far to port as the guys would safely take it. The maximum amount of buoy chain was visible, the shackle between buoy bridle and mooring chain about a fathom above the rolled angle of deck and side.

Above all their heads the five tons of the buoy shone wetly, swaying slightly backwards and forwards as *Active* rolled gently. The clank and drag of chain links marked a flurry of activity below the buoy as a gang of men dragged the slack of the gangway chain from the capstan across to the rail. They lifted the last fathom of it while the leading man shackled it to the almost vertical buoy mooring that led above their heads. The suspended buoy dripped copiously upon them. The shackle pin went home and they simultaneously let go of the chain and ran clear. Immediately the main capstan began to turn, winding in the slack and then snatching at the mooring chain. At the same time Hobden lowered the buoy to the deck. A few minutes later the buoy was disconnected and *Active* lay safely to the buoy's mooring and waited to recover the sinker after the buoy itself had been lashed down. Naismith ordered the helm amidships and checked the tachometers. The engines were stopped and the propellers turned slowly in the tide.

"Now what does his lordship astern want, eh?"

What his lordship wanted was permission to board, and a few minutes later, conveyed by Zodiac inflatable, a young Naval lieutenant in life-preserver and blue, epauletted anorak entered *Active*'s wheelhouse. He brought his hand up to the beret in a courteous, though casual salute.

"Morning, sir, Lieutenant Elliott . . ."

"Good morning Lieutenant, Captain Naismith. What can we do for you?"

"Er, my captain's compliments, sir and would you be so kind as to confiscate the films from the several people on board this ship who took photographs of

Harwich." It was not a request, it was a crudely disguised order.

Naismith looked at the fresh young face with some astonishment. His glance slid sideways to Third Officer Sobey who, caught redhanded unshipping his telephoto lens, flushed hotly.

"I beg your pardon, Lieutenant, but do I understand you correctly? You wish *me* to confiscate private property?"

The lieutenant nodded.

"I still don't understand, Mr Elliott. We have seen a great number of pictures of your ship in recent months. I imagine my crew wanted their own record of her, I cannot see that a few snapshots pose any great threat to national security, mmm?" Elliott swallowed, feeling the ball fall heavily in his court. He considered for a moment then stepped forward. "May I have a word privately, sir?"

Naismith nodded and led the way out onto the bridge wing. From the foredeck they heard the mate's bellow. "Ready to weigh sinker!"

Naismith leaned over the bridge wing and nodded then he turned to Elliott.

"Now, Mr Elliott . . .?"

"I'm sorry, sir, but it is a matter of some sensitivity . . ." Naismith bridled at that increasingly familiar euphemism. He wondered what exactly it was a euphemism for.

"Would you mind telling me exactly why, Mr Elliott? Is it a matter of *Harwich* or the wreck down there?" He pointed overside.

"I'm sorry sir," said Elliott firmly, as though Naismith had pushed the matter beyond negotiation, "I must insist."

"Look Lieutenant, a lot of my men admired what

the navy did in the Falklands. A lot of them have just come back from their holidays and have end-of-roll exposures left in their cameras. Now you want me to confiscate those films in a rather Draconian act that will only bring down trouble at the next Trade Union meeting. I'm sorry but I am not prepared to do it on your behalf, particularly as you have not the courtesy to offer me an explanation. Now, you may use my VHF to speak with your CO, but you will not coerce me into spoiling my crew's films in this way." He held his hand out and ushered the lieutenant back into the wheelhouse.

"Sinker's awa-a-ay!" Hobden shouted. Naismith rang the engines dead slow.

"Keep her steady as you go, quartermaster."

"Steady as she goes, sir."

Lieutenant Elliott was hunched over the VHF. Naismith did not try to eavesdrop, though he heard "won't cooperate" and "awkward", though whether the last applied to the situation or to his own obduracy he did not know. He rather hoped the latter. He was getting a little fed up with people complicating the running of his ship.

Elliott straightened up from the VHF. "Would you object to accompanying me to *Harwich*, captain?"

Naismith frowned with sudden alarm and something in his expression must have communicated itself to Elliott. To the young lieutenant the gaunt master of the *Active* looked, if not conforming to the Dartmouth model, at least a man he would not care to cross at his present stage on the navy list. Naismith recovered his composure.

"I trust you are not forcing me off my ship, Lieutenant; that is piracy you know."

Lieutenant Elliott did not know whether it was

piracy or not. He had served in fishery protection cruisers and manned dashing boarding parties over the rails of many trawlers, but such activity had acquired the sanctity of usage. The hostility of the fishermen was professional and abusive, but largely impersonal. The atmosphere on *Active*'s bridge was demonstrably hostile; the quartermaster stood, wooden-faced at the wheel; Mr Sobey still held his camera as if uncertain what to do with it.

"Good heavens, sir, it's just that I think my captain should have a word with you," he elocuted in a belated tone of amiability.

"Very well." Naismith leaned over the bridge wing and called Hobden to the wheelhouse. The mate arrived, massive, bearded and forbidding, his protective boots and boiler suit incongruous in the brass-shiny place with its quiet, insistent electronic hums. "My first officer, Mr Hobden, Lieutenant Elliott from HMS *Harwich*."

"Pleased to meet you."

Hobden grunted and gave his filthy hand only a perfunctory wipe before crushing the naval officer's fist.

"Chas, take over will you. I've been summoned to *Harwich*. She's dead slow ahead into the tide on oh-six-five."

"Aye, aye, sir, oh-six-five."

Naismith led the way to the companionway, then stopped and Elliott only just avoided bumping into him. "By the way Chas, if I'm not back in half an hour, send a boarding party . . ."

Elliott followed the captain down, Hobden's laughter ringing in his ears. He felt he was the butt end of an uncomprehended joke.

*   *   *

"Drink?" Captain Troughton was a dark, well groomed and very typical naval officer. Naismith had expected no less and he accepted the whisky and water gracefully. He recognised immediately that Troughton had his own problems and he outlined his unwillingness to comply with Elliott's ultimatum.

"I see," said Troughton when he had finished. "Bit of an impasse, eh?"

"Look Captain, there is a way round the matter and if you'd oblige me with the barest explanation of why this damned wreck is so *sensitive* I'll do my best to oblige. To be frank I've been buggered about with this job and I'm bloody curious."

"Well, we've cleared all the trailing ropes off it, so I don't think it presents any threat to navigation," said Troughton blandly. "Once the buoy's gone you can proceed on your way. Truth to tell I had hoped to be away from the thing myself before you arrived, but we struck a bit of bad luck and got delayed." Naismith frowned. So *Active* was not supposed to have arrived on the scene to remove the buoy until after *Harwich* had left . . .

"We *have* cleared the ropes, Captain," offered Troughton. "Saved you a job . . ."

"Hardly, we were ordered to abandon our diving operation . . ."

"You mean you had a diver on the wreck?" asked Troughton sharply. He was clearly surprised. Naismith nodded, a little quiver of excitement fluttering in the pit of his stomach. He had the feeling of being close to a mystery. "*Harwich*'s a big ship to send on a simple diving mission, Captain," he said as Troughton considered the matter.

"What? Oh, er, we were handy, Captain, that's all."

He paused, looking intently at Naismith. "Did your diver report anything unusual?"

Naismith felt the acute observation of an intelligent brain. He looked squarely at Troughton. "He found the location of two more of the missing crew, one was the woman, the master's wife I believe, the third was probably in the engine room."

Troughton nodded. "He *was* in the engine room. We brought them all out."

"You went to a lot of trouble."

Troughton ignored the sarcasm. "Anything else?"

Naismith raised his eyebrows and pulled his face into an expression of casual negation. "Nnn-no, not really. A few dust carts on deck and a deck cargo of drums."

Naismith caught the smallest of contractions in the tiny but highly reactive muscles about Troughton's eyes. He knew instinctively that Troughton would not himself volunteer information so he prodded a little, remembering Scranton's report. "The drums were above the point of impact. I understand that the bulwark was destroyed in way of the stow and some of them had fallen to the seabed . . ." He knew he had caught Troughton's interest now.

"You are well briefed, captain," said Troughton drily but Naismith would not be drawn and continued:

"I presume you wish to recover some, er, *sensitive* portion of *Wallenstein*'s cargo." He sighed. Troughton's silence was becoming oppressively melodramatic. "Oh, for God's sake, Captain Troughton, I'm no child. I've been in cargo ships, kept the lifelines open with plastic flowers and trannies from Hong Kong all through the sixties and I've even signed the Official Secrets Act . . ."

Troughton suddenly smiled, a surprisingly frank and pleasant smile considering he had just been shouted at in his own cabin.

"I'm sorry, Captain," he took Naismith's glass and refilled it, "I hate all this bloody cloak-and-dagger stuff." He took a swallow and Naismith did not miss the quick look at the enlarged coloured photograph of a lean grey shape surrounded by near-miss bomb splashes: *Harwich* in San Carlos water. He sensed a sadness and regret that Troughton's moment had come and gone in those few weeks of 1982.

"You are quite right, there is an item of cargo on board *Wallenstein* in which we are interested. We had hoped to get it earlier, as I said, but we haven't located it yet. I suppose your diver didn't bring anything up did he?"

Naismith shook his head. "Only a lifebuoy to identify the ship."

"Nothing else? No drums, boxes, souvenirs?"

"No." Naismith was still puzzled. "If you haven't found your whatever it is, Captain, why d'you want my lads to lose their holiday snaps?"

"You were going to tell me how we could get over the problem of them," Troughton said evasively; he had come to the end of the line. He would not be drawn further.

"I will collect all the films. If you undertake to process them and return all pictures not contravening whatever rule you are invoking, I think I can persuade my lads to agree." Naismith knew that all of *Active's* crew would already know why he had been called to the warship, a fact he hoped would make his task easier when he returned. He was pleased to see Troughton smiling.

"Excellent suggestion, Captain, and I do apologise for making a fuss but it is a little . . ."

"Sensitive?"

"Yes, exactly."

Naismith smiled and held out his hand as he stood up. "Thank you for being sympathetic . . ." Troughton rang the bridge and a bright young sub-lieutenant came down to shepherd Naismith back to the waiting Zodiac.

They emerged onto the port-side upper deck and walked aft. Naismith recognised the nature of the long plastic bundles that lay in wire stretchers along the outboard rail. He was also aware of a gang of men lashing an old tarpaulin over a stow of something on the flight deck. He recognised the shape instantly and crossed the deck to lift a corner of the flapping tarpaulin.

"You there!" Naismith ignored the command. All he could see on the drums was a chemical company logo and the stencilled words; *Dry cleaning fluid.*

"What the hell d'you think you're doing?"

Naismith looked up at the lieutenant commander, *Harwich*'s first lieutenant.

"Being nosey, Commander . . . good day to you . . ."

He headed for the ladder, passing the escorting sub-lieutenant who was clearly going to pay for his own importunity.

Naismith sat in the Zodiac and let the tight-lipped divers run him back to his ship. He had solved part of the mystery. Troughton had relaxed and changed the subject the instant he knew *Active* had not recovered any drums. The first lieutenant had nearly burst a blood vessel when he saw the unmilitary person of James Naismith peering under that tarpaulin.

It was not *Harwich* that Troughton did not want photographed, it was those drums. And *Harwich*'s divers had failed to find all of them.

So whatever was in those drums was politically "sensitive". They were not supposed to exist and whatever *was* in them it was not dry cleaning fluid. But what the devil was it? As Susan was so fond of telling them, governments did not care what substances polluted the sea.

Or did they?

Chapter Eight

Susan had been turned in during the recovery of the buoy and the captain's visit to *Harwich*. When she was called, however, they had not dropped the warship below the horizon due to the delay occasioned in collecting all the films. Several men still had unused exposures and, at the prospect of having the Ministry of Defence pay for the processing, ran the films off on their shipmates acting the fool. This light-hearted conclusion to the incident made Naismith's task simple. Since the Falklands campaign, military necessity had been quietly accepted by the populace at large and seamen in particular. While Naismith might deplore that circumstance privately, he had to acknowledge the recovery of the films and prospective loss of a few snaps did not seem to bother anybody. The ship still buzzed with talk of the morning's events and it was not long before Susan was acquainted with all the facts from one source or another.

As she sat in the saloon she listened with increasing interest to Naismith's account of his visit to *Harwich*. At the time he revealed very little, speaking in general terms and admitting that the destroyer was diving on the wreck in order to recover something. He also took refuge in the fact that the photographs of *Harwich* were "sensitive", suppressing a wry grin as he did so as no one else would understand the joke. He was rescued from any real breach of faith with either Troughton or the Official Secrets Act by the third engineer, Colin Mulliner.

"It's probably because of the new Phalanx anti-missile defense systems they've just fitted to the Type 42s," he said knowledgeably. There was a general nod of agreement round the table.

"Odd that they went to all that trouble, though," added Hobden, "when you think of all the photographs that have appeared since the Falklands Campaign."

"Yes, well you see, Chas," said Mulliner patiently, "these Phalanx systems have been fitted as a response to the Exocet attacks . . . ."

But Susan was not listening. She chewed her roast pork ruminatively. The interest of the warship in the wreck was undoubtedly unusual. It was not even a British ship that lay on the sea bed. But the main fact was that *Harwich* was not the first warship to show an interest. There had been that submarine.

"D'you think that the *Harwich*'s visit has anything to do with that submarine, sir?" She addressed the remark quietly across Hobden's back as the mate leaned forward to put Mr Colin bloody Mulliner firmly in his place and ensure that the unfortunate fellow did not make the mistake a second time of taking Charles Hobden for an ignorant fool. Susan watched Naismith's face. He had just taken a mouthful of food and for a second he sat with his lips closed but his jaws apart as he remembered the circumstance.

Naismith *had* forgotten the submarine. Called in the middle of the night and finding the odd sonar echo the only reason for his broken sleep he had dismissed the matter, retired to bed and fallen asleep immediately. Susan had not pressed it, feeling that Potts' adamant attitude had somehow compromised her, and had also not raised the question the next day. The absolute identification of the sonar trace as a submarine had actually only been registered by Potts, Susan merely half-believing it and Naismith dismissing it utterly.

But as he ate, Naismith realised with total certainty that it *had* been a submarine. And what further interested him was whether it was a British boat or a foreigner. If it had been the latter, might it not have taken those drums for which Troughton was now searching? And if *that* was the case, governments might be implicated and the whole incident be one of much greater moment than mere pollution.

Naismith finished his mouthful and swallowed. He nodded at Susan. "Quite right, Susan, that's very possible . . ." But for the moment he did not want to enlarge, he wanted very much to think.

The ratings,' mess had already come to the same conclusion, well in advance of the officers. Potts, rising late like Susan made the connection as soon as he heard about the morning's excitement. Although he knew nothing about the drums, he was absolutely sure that the nocturnal visitor had been a submarine. He spent some time explaining to the big messroom the circumstances of the incident and ended with his candid opinion of the Old Man's total incompetence in the particular field of sonar identification.

"Whatever's in that fucking wreck, then, must be valuable, eh?" said Harris, his eyes gleaming.

"Don't you ever think of anything except cunt and money, Harris . . .?"

"Well it could be gold, like the fucking *Edinburgh*. They're getting the stuff out of the *Lusitania*, or trying

109

to aren't they? Anyway what makes you sneer at gold, Pottsy, eh?"

"Politics," said Potts obscurely, aware that as quartermaster, in close touch with the bridge, he had a tremendous advantage over the mere jack-arsed deckhands.

"What d'you mean 'politics', eh? What's fucking politics got to do with it?"

"Look, why don't you think a bit? Ask yourself why the navy's interested enough to send a submarine to find the wreck without anyone else knowing, and then a diving team to salvage some of its cargo? Then ask yourself, what is it that would cause trouble somewhere, wherever this ship what's sunk is going, and then what might that ship be carrying to cause that trouble in that particular place and what have you got, eh?" Potts leaned back, enjoying himself.

Harris was discomfitted. "The bleeding house that Jack built, by the sound of it."

"An H-Bomb!" shouted Ellice in sudden comprehension, "A fucking H-Bomb!"

Potts smiled at Harris' total lack of brains. "The lad's all there, mate, see?"

"No I don't see," replied Harris sullenly. "How d'you know if the ship what sunk's got an H-Bomb on her? D'you think they'd send one of them round the bleeding world without all sorts of bloody precautions?" An expression of contempt crossed Harris' face. Don't be daft. You know fuck all, Pottsy . . ."

"How d'you think they move them about then? Eh? They don't get from where they're made to where they're going with a bloody great escort do they, or those bloody long-haired left-wing bastards would be screaming blue murder at them," Potts replied with

110

ponderous certainty. "Don't forget I've been in the navy, mate, and I've seen some of the things that go on. No, they ship them aboard merchant ships as something else and off they go . . ."

Harris fell silent. Since no one knew any better, no one contradicted him. They had accepted Potts' explanation as being logical and probable. The image of a nuclear bomb lying in *Wallenstein*'s hold struck them all with varying degrees of imaginative force. Potts drove his advantage home.

"Remember the bloody fuss the Yanks made a few years back when they lost one off Spain?"

"Christ, aye . . ."

"Pottsy . . .?" said Ellice uncertainly, not liking the silence that had fallen over a normally noisy messroom. "D'you know where that ship was going? The wreck I mean?"

Potts tossed off his half-pint mug of tea and stood up. "Course I do," he said, aware that Ellice's correct guess had not exactly followed the path he had himself outlined.

"Central America, Santa Maria de los Mayas . . ."

"Where?" They all turned, surprised at the sudden vehement reaction from the hitherto silent seaman on the next table. Potts, who had been embroiled with his own manoeuvring to put Harris down, had forgotten the coincidence of which second officer Paulin had told him. He remembered it now as Frank Davis rose, white-faced, from the adjacent table. "Where?" he repeated, whispering now.

They had left him to himself since he had the news of his son's death. Grief was a personal matter and although one or two of the older men had offered a word of comfort to him, their communal act of condolence had been one of silence.

Able-seaman Harris looked at the newcomer. A sexually indiscriminate person, he had nevertheless expressed his contempt for Brits marrying 'dagos'. In his view the photograph of Davis' wife showed that, though she might prove a good screw, she was definitely a dago.

"Santa Maria, mate," he said, "they're thinking about nukeing all the dagos there."

No one stopped Davis as he hit Harris. It was only when he had knocked the man to the deck and had his hands on Harris' throat that they pulled him off. And when the bosun came down to find out who had laid Harris up for the afternoon they knew nothing at all about it.

Davis was not the only person in the mess deck to overhear the conversation. At a forward table, bored and idle, the two divers Scranton and Walker nursed the latest in a series of mugs of tea, the drinking of which had been their chief occupation since the helicopter left them stranded aboard *Active*.

"Stupid bastards," muttered Walker contemptuously, dismissing the conversation of the seamen.

Scranton's reaction was rather different. He pricked up his ears, saying nothing, but leaving the half drunk mug of tea and going in search of Naismith. Left alone, Walker sighed, then stood up and left the mess, bound for the tiny "spare" cabin he and Scranton occupied and the stack of "girlie" magazines that were the only literature he favoured. Both divers had left the mess deck before the fight.

Scranton found Naismith in his cabin, reading some papers and trying to sort out the chaos of his desk. His heart was not in it and he had come to an almost identical conclusion as the ratings, except that he knew the navy were not chasing H-Bombs, merely drums, dark green drums of "cleaning fluid". Perhaps, had he been able to conclude the quarry was something as straightforward as a mere nuclear device in transit, something he and the rest of the world apparently tolerated as a necessary evil, he would have been able to concentrate on the tedious paperwork. Nuclear weapons existed whether he, or any other "ordinary" person liked it or not. There was nothing to be done about it. Like a thousand and one other evils that mankind had loosed upon the planet. He thought of the dolphins and of the slow death by poisoning they were being subjected to. The thought brought him back to Susan Paulin and her one-woman antipollution campaign. Well, he had to admit to himself, he admired her and her single-mindedness. There was an honesty about it that had an intelligence quite at variance with that of Captain Troughton. And so he came full circle to the drums upon *Harwich*'s deck. But beyond a vague unease that their contents were sinister, he was no nearer solving the mystery.

At this point in his reverie Scranton knocked on his cabin door.

"Can I have a word with you, Captain Naismith?"

Naismith was relieved to see Scranton was devoid of a bottle. He was less happy about the concern on Scranton's face that spoke of some problem brought to Naismith for solution. On top of his other preoccupations Naismith felt it was all getting a bit ridiculous.

"Hullo, Mr Scranton. If it's about getting you ashore, don't worry. We're on our way east now. I'm bound to drop these buoys on deck off at the Goodwins and can land you at Dover. Okay?"

Scranton shook his head. "No, it's not that Captain. Mr Hobden told us your intentions. Dover'll be fine. No, I wanted a word in confidence."

"In confidence?" Naismith did not want another confession, but he said, "What is it?"

"It's about the *Wallenstein*, Captain. I think you ought to know what really happened down there." Scranton paused. "Mind if I sit down . . .?"

"N . . . no, no go ahead." Naismith turned his chair. A sensation of apprehension crawled down his spine. Scranton sat on the edge of the easy-chair.

"It's about the *Wallenstein*," he repeated.

"What exactly?" Naismith asked cautiously.

"There's something odd about that wreck, isn't there?"

"Well. I . . . er, I'm not sure . . ."

"Come on Captain, we're not children. Your seamen down below think she was carrying hydrogen bombs out to Costa Maya. The presence of that bloody destroyer was unusual, so was confiscating the films after you were hauled over to the naval ship. Eh? It all looks pretty bloody sinister doesn't it?"

Naismith nodded. It was stupid to try and maintain any kind of detachment from the events of the last few days. There was something odd about the wreck and whether he liked it or not *Active* had become involved.

"Yes, Mr Scranton. There is something odd about the wreck. I'm not sure what . . ." he hedged a little, not mentioning the drums, but Scranton burst out.

"Well I am, Captain. It's drums of some kind of chemical or other and I'd say that the navy was diving on the wreck to recover those drums."

Naismith frowned. He wondered whether Scranton had seen the drums on *Harwich*'s deck; and although he had mentioned drums as forming part of the *Wallenstein*'s deck cargo, it had been a casual reference. There was nothing unusual in a ship carrying such a consignment on her open decks.

"What makes you sure that it was drums they were after?" he asked. "And why are these drums so very special?"

Scranton was perspiring and clearly under a lot of stress. "Look Captain, I suppose that I should have told you before, but frankly I didn't want to get involved. Now that the whole thing is apparently bigger than I imagined, it's going to look bloody odd if you don't know what I came across while I was down there."

"What the hell are you talking about?"

"For Christ's sake, I'm telling you that you should know what I came across, in case . . . well, I'll be in the shit if you don't know . . ."

It occurred to Naismith that whatever was on Scranton's mind might have made a lot of difference to the conduct of the interview aboard *Harwich*. It was too late for Scranton to confess now, otherwise it would look as if he, Naismith, had withheld information. It might be better not to know, to pretend Scranton had never seen whatever it was and avoid the necessity of being compelled to cover for him. But Scranton wanted the relief of the confessional.

"Look, Captain I saw a dead man down there. Not a dead seaman. A dead diver."

"A dead diver?"

"Yes. One reason I didn't tell you at the time was because it was pretty unsettling."

"Unsettling?" It seemed an odd word to use but Naismith remembered Scranton's condition the night he had been drunk. "Go on."

"He was wearing standard British Admiralty diving gear . . . scuba gear . . . he was caught in the rigging and had died in agony. There wasn't anything left of his hands. They had been eaten away . . ."

"Eaten away?"

Scranton nodded. "Yes. Below him on the deck were a few drums. The rest were scattered on the seabed. One of the drums left on deck had been crushed and opened by a section of the ship's bulwarks where they had been torn in the collision."

"That's a bit circumstantial . . ."

"I suppose you're going to suggest it was fucking piranha fish in the English Channel," Scranton exploded in exasperation. "I'm telling you, Captain Naismith that a British naval diver died from some kind of poisoning from a barrel carried aboard that ship. He had obviously got entangled in the rigging around the mast as he tried to get to the surface."

"But where did he come from?"

"Jesus Captain, the whole bloody ship knows there was a submarine on that wreck the previous night."

"Christ!" said Naismith going pale with sudden realisation that his own preoccupation with pollution had blinded him to the obvious. "I'd forgotten all about that."

A silence filled the cabin. Naismith rose and opened a locker. He pulled out two glasses and a bottle of Scotch. "My turn, I think." He poured a generous measure into each glass and handed one to Scranton.

"What d'you think was in those drums?" he asked.

Scranton shrugged. "My guess is some kind of highly toxic industrial chemical. Something so bloody poisonous that the government don't want it polluting the Channel."

Naismith nodded. "You haven't had any ill-effects?"

"Eh?"

"The water must have been clear when you dived. You haven't suffered any ill-effects?"

"No. Leastways not like that. But I'll not forget the way that poor bastard looked. Christ, it was horrible. I put my torch on his face. It was kind of purple, with eruptions . . ."

"If," said Naismith slowly, the image of the diver dying an agonising death beneath *Active*'s hull while he testily went back to bed, fixing itself reproachfully in his imagination, "if he was a naval diver, wouldn't he have had a mate? I mean you work in pairs . . ."

Scranton nodded and put down an empty glass. Naismith refilled it. "Yes, of course, and the other bloke, when he saw what had happened probably took off like a rocket. The bloke who died might have warned him off. Anyway it explains the reason why that destroyer was there. The navy would want the body back once the tide had swept the area clear."

"Yes." Naismith swallowed the second whisky. "Have you told anyone else?"

Scranton looked pained. "How the hell could I? I should have reported the corpse, but for some reason the sight of that chap scared me shitless. He's not the first I've seen, by a long chalk, but when you see your own cloth . . . like that . . ." He paused and tossed off the second glass. "I'm getting a bit old, Captain. My nerve was shaken a bit, that's why I made a fool of myself in here the other night . . ." He paused again, as though the recollection and the retelling caused him anguish. "Maybe I was just telling myself I could still take it . . ."

"So Walker doesn't know?" Naismith persisted,

117

aware that he was somehow involved and wanting to know all the facts before he was asked anything else from any other Captain Troughtons.

"Walker? That popinjay! Good God, no!"

"And you only told me because you should have reported the matter?"

Scranton nodded. "Well, yes. You're nominally in charge of the operation. I'm supposed to file a diving report. The standard form is that I dived in accordance with your instructions. Saves me a lot of tedious writing." He stopped again and Naismith refilled his glass, sensing the man wanted to say something else.

"And . . ."

"I made a fool of myself didn't I? I suppose I wanted you to know . . . to know that . . ." Scranton was heaving the words out with great difficulty. Naismith suddenly realised that the man's moral dissolution was already well advanced before he got anywhere near the *Wallenstein*. ". . . To know that I hadn't gone soft." Scranton swallowed the whisky and sighed, like a man making a deathbed confession of an old murder.

Naismith looked at him in silence. If there was anything more to the matter, and the contents of his conversation with Troughton became known, it would be assumed that Scranton had already told him about the presence of the dead diver. It would appear that he had withheld that information from the naval officer, or that Scranton had not seen the dead man. The second option would tally with the events as they occurred, but it meant Scranton and he would now have to conceal the information. On the other hand the first option compromised himself rather. Naismith sighed. Of course they could tell the truth, but that would look bad for Scranton. Naismith rubbed his chin reflectively. He had told Troughton there had been a diver down from *Active*. To the best of his recollection Troughton had asked if any drums, boxes or souvenirs had been recovered. He had replied in the negative, with the exception of an identifying life buoy. Troughton had mentioned nothing about the body of a diver. Why? There were three of *Wallenstein*'s crew known to be missing and Scranton himself had seen a woman and the radio officer still trapped inside the accommodation. Should not Troughton have asked . . .? No, he recollected Troughton had said they had "got them all out". Naismith had passed them on the deck; the plastic bundles in those sinister wire stretchers.

And there had been four of them!

He could not imagine why he had not thought of it before. Like the presence of the submarine it fitted so well and he had forgotten it! Well he was a shipmaster, not a damned detective.

"Look, Mr Scranton," he said after a while, "you'll have to do a bit of writing, I'm afraid. Put in a full report, mention all the bodies you saw and say recovery was made impossible by the tide getting away, eh? I imagine that isn't far from the truth, is it? After all, we were prevented from returning and completing the job, weren't we?"

Naismith saw the relief plain on Scranton's face.

"Thank you, Captain." He rose and held out his hand. Naismith had the curious sensation that he should not take the proffered hand, that to do so was to acknowledge his involvement in some half-comprehended conspiracy. But he dismissed the idea as a whisky-induced fancy, as whisky-induced as Scranton's gesture.

"I won't mention the drums down below, Captain.

I think it's best they think the navy were looking for an H-bomb."

Naismith smiled. "I think you're probably right, Mr Scranton."

As the door curtain dropped behind the retreating diver Naismith put the whisky bottle away. He wished he had not drunk such big pegs so rapidly, but they were on passage and he could put his feet up and doze for an hour.

He settled himself on his settee and closed his eyes. The image of the dead diver swam into his mind's eye and he turned the conversations with Troughton and Scranton over and over, wondering what it all really had to do with him.

It was a coincidence that the *Wallenstein* had been on passage to Santa Maria where Able Seaman Davis's wife lived, it was ludicrous that the ratings thought she was carrying a hydrogen bomb, it was pitiful that Scranton was on the verge of losing his nerve and it was reprehensible that he had forgotten about that damned submarine. But somehow it was simply none of his business, even if his second officer did keep lecturing them all about pollution.

And it occurred to him in a brief moment of extreme prejudice, that none of these ridiculous thoughts would have troubled him if *Active*'s second officer had not been a young woman.

Chapter Nine

Captain James Naismith looked over the side as the orange mooring ropes hauled *Active*'s bulk sideways against the quay. The *Wallenstein* affair had shrunk in his conscious mind and was reduced officially to a three-page report, some echo sounder and sonar traces, the latter of which were already dry and faded.

He picked up the handset and called, "In position, make her all-fast." He looked forward once more to where Sobey acknowledged with a wave and then aft to where he could see Susan, her Wren officer-type hat rakishly over one eye, staring forward and telling the shore gang to take out extra stern-ropes. He suppressed a smile. He knew they pretended not to understand in order to provoke her to an outburst of unfeminine language. He turned into the wheelhouse. He made a final entry in the log book, signed it and nodded to the quartermaster who telegraphed "finished with engines" to the engine room.

He went below, scooped up the documents assembled for his collection and made for the half-rigged gangway where he met Hobden.

"Get those dirty Goodwin buoys ashore, Chas, I'll confirm what's to load but I imagine it's that lot on the quay. If so, get it on board and secured."

"Aye, aye, sir."

The seamen rigging the gangway moved silently aside for him. He knew they wanted a run ashore and the unasked question of whether they were going to get one hung heavy in the air.

He walked briskly through the vast buoy-yard with its stores, smithy, piles of chains, sinkers and painted and rusty buoys to the administrative offices of BNAS.

The superintendent was on the phone and motioned him to a seat. Naismith ignored the conversation, glancing about himself abstractedly and smiling at Joyce Faraday, Campbell's personal assistant who suffered from a plain face but an extraordinarily voluptuous figure that never failed to quicken his pulse after a week or two at sea.

"Hullo, Captain," she said, well aware of the effect she had. Naismith managed a roguish wink which he hoped convinced Miss Faraday that he was still on the potent side of forty.

"Well, *Active*'s just berthed and Captain Naismith is sitting opposite me. D'you want to speak to him . . .? All right I will pass that on . . . very well . . . yes, I quite understand, but you must realise that Naismith is not in possession of the facts and was only acting in a conscientious manner . . . very well . . . Goodbye."

The phone went down with a slam and Campbell got up and lit a cigarette.

"What the bloody hell have you been doing to upset the navy, James? That was the Chief Executive himself wanting to know why the Ministry of Defence have a bill for thirty-two quid and a complaint against you for non-cooperation."

Naismith outlined the nature of his interview with Troughton and the circumstances that led up to it. "I had no idea Troughton was going to sling shit when he got back to Pompey, or Portland, or wherever the hell he ended up. This is bloody irritating . . ."

"Calm down, James. We don't know that Troughton did, only that some bloke in MOD has rung up the Chief Exec. and complained about the bill and some non-cooperation. The Chief's probably hung up about the last part while the MOD man is going over the top about thirty-two pounds that he's got no way of paying by a standard method and generates a lot of paperwork. Apart from being a bit bloody-minded I'd say that you hadn't been entirely unreasonable. You got our chaps to cooperate, that speaks for itself." He grinned. "You say you parted on friendly terms with this naval chap Troughton?"

Naismith nodded. "Perfectly. I was a bit curt with his young lieutenant, but then I don't like being told what to do by a boy *and* on my own bridge."

Campbell smiled. "You're telling me."

Naismith coloured. "Damn it, sir, I don't like being kept in the dark. All this fencing about . . ."

"Talking about prejudices," interrupted Campbell, "how's *Ms* Paulin settling down?"

"Fine. She's a very professional officer. Now what was that bloody ship carrying?"

Campbell sighed, sat down and lit a second cigarette from the first. "You know that much do you . . ."

"That much was obvious even to a fish-headed jolly jack like me."

"James, I would tell you if I could, but the fact of the matter is that I don't know myself. All I've done is act as messenger boy, and that I'm in trouble too."

"You are?" Naismith was surprised. "Why is that?"

"Because I was supposed to signal you to tell you to delay leaving Falmouth because . . ."

"*Harwich* hadn't found what she was looking for and wasn't clear of the area."

Campbell nodded through a haze of smoke. "Hole in one, James."

"Oh, that's bloody stupid. Any number of merchant ships passed her while she was sitting there."

"Yes, but it's not unusual for a British warship to be in the English Channel, is it? It's about the only place we're allowed to have 'em nowadays."

Naismith sighed. "Yes, I suppose you're right, but it rather presupposes that *Active* spells trouble, doesn't it?"

"It rather looks as if they might've been right too," Campbell said drily.

"Well, why didn't you send the message?" Naismith was beginning to long for the open air again. Offices tended to make him irritably unreasonable, particularly when he felt his ship was being criticised.

"Because," said Campbell, raising his eyebrows in an admission of mock guilt, "I was halfway down the sixteenth fairway on a better-than-average round and I had left my bleeper in the car, the car in the garage and had walked to the golf club to keep my coronary at bay. Instead I shall die of a perforated ulcer and God grant that it be not too long delayed so that you can come in here and answer this sodding telephone . . ." Campbell snatched up the clamorous instrument.

He picked up a sheet of paper and handed it to Naismith. "Your orders, James . . . Hullo, Campbell here . . ." He waved Naismith out of the office with a lopsided grin.

It was only then that Naismith realised that he had not pointed out Scranton's report among his own papers. Oh, well. The matter seemed to have blown over. He supposed *Harwich*'s first lieutenant must have got rather annoyed over the business of the drums under the tarpaulin. That was obviously "uncooperative" and the matter would most certainly have been reported to Troughton.

Naismith paused in the buoy-yard to read his orders. They were to load the buoys on the quay and take a lightvessel under tow for a station in the Channel. He was to retain the divers on board and they were to inspect the moorings already on the seabed.

He could have done without another week of Scranton's lugubrious company.

Naismith settled in front of the small portable television in his cabin. He had decided to sail early the following morning and stem the flood tide as he towed the lightvessel out of the harbour. Apart from the harbour watch, *Active*'s hands were already ashore and drinking their second pints of beer.

The newscaster completed reading an item concerning an industrial dispute in the Midlands and announced a correspondent's report that had Naismith instantly attentive.

Gunships over jungle. It might have been Vietnam again except that a tanned and indomitable girl-reporter in sawn-off denims and a dentally ethnic necklace said it was Central America.

". . . Although there was no evidence of it during the government patrol over the jungles and plantations to the west of the capital, Santa Maria de los Mayas, and we landed at a village firmly in the hands of government forces . . ." There was a vast dust cloud and the outline of automatic weapons and US-style steel helmets, then a close up of a school class. Naismith thought of Davis and his lovely wife. He tried to remember her name as the nasal American voice went on. ". . . There are reports coming in from sources in neighbouring countries where the refugee problem is becoming acute, that the government is using chemical warfare against the peasant population. This is categorically denied by military and presidential sources. They are claiming a government-ordered build-down of military forces, stating that allegations of this kind are Communist-inspired anti-government propaganda. Although counter-insurgency operations are still in force in remote areas, a high-ranking military source in Santa Maria told me today, the use of chemical weapons would be counterproductive . . ."

"That's not a denial . . ." Naismith muttered.

The picture changed. In front of what he assumed to be the presidential palace the same girl, dressed now in a silk blouse and jeans continued. "Whatever the truth of these claims and counter-claims it appears that the suburb of Santiago, the dockland area of Santa Maria which was taken a week ago by anti-government rebels, has now been cleared of insurgents and is back in government hands . . ." A high-speed patrol hurried through the streets of an obvious dockland area. Naismith had an image of Davis and his wife walking hand in hand, but the place was deserted. ". . . And the army patrols pass in perfect safety. Presidential sources claimed that destabilising elements have been trained by revolutionary governments sympathetic to world Communism and it looks to its main ally, the United States, for support. This is Sally Blumthal, NBC News, Santa Maria de los Mayas."

The picture changed again, reverting to the bland BBC newsreader in London.

"In support of the allegations contained in that

NCB report a West German film team has sent these pictures from refugee camps on the Costa Mayan borders."

The screen filled with a sea of misery, mostly women and children, weary, tattered and hungry. "Refugees are said to be leaving Costa Maya at some three or four hundred a day and they are telling stories of fierce fighting throughout the country . . ." The camera suddenly, appallingly, closed in on a woman with a child in her arms. At least that was what Naismith supposed it was. The figure sat against a wooden shed and her face was obscene, the flesh yellowed and blistered, her eyes invisible behind the puffed-up flesh, her shoulders purulent, a mass of flies and sticking strands of hair. Her child was indescribable.

Naismith stared, sickened. "Christ Almighty . . ." He got up and switched off the television, then stood uncertainly before it, rubbing his chin.

He felt overwhelmed by a sense of self-disgust, that he was a party to the real obscenity he had just witnessed. His cultivated cynicism was swept aside as he saw that woman and her child again in his mind's eye. It was an ancient image; the Madonna and the infant Christ, the salvation of mankind . . .

But it had been violated, converted at a stroke to an image of infinite horror with a deliberation that rocked the reason. Naismith found himself shaking with an impotent anger. He was part of this evil, part of this mutant species called humanity whose brain had developed too quickly, whose skeleton was still that of a quadruped yet whose wayward brilliance could destroy itself like no other creature on earth.

Then from his anger he began to realise his self-disgust had a more personal cause. It was beginning to dawn on him that he was the recipient of a number of facts directly concerned with the thing he had just witnessed on the television. Perhaps he was the sole recipient, the only person outside the conspiracy who was party to a horror that made him physically sick. The evidence was circumstantial, conjectural, even, he realised with a jolt, providential, for the television news seemed to confirm it.

He knew what was on board the *Wallenstein* now; why there was a tremendous fuss to recover it. The string of coincidences; of Davis' presence on the *Active*, of his personal life, the submarine, the dead diver and Scranton's dilatory report, the intervention of Troughton, all fell logically into place. Even Susan's desire to convert *Active*'s master to the committed anti-pollution lobby seemed not to be fortuitous.

He sat down, still trembling. Those covered drums on *Harwich*'s deck with the crook-legged logo had not been dry-cleaning fluid. Neither had they been the industrial chemical Scranton had supposed.

They were a concentrated agent of nerve gas.

Chapter Ten

Naismith was tired and irritable as he looked astern from the starboard bridge wing. He had slept badly and the operation of taking the lightvessel in tow had been slow. Most of the crew appeared to be suffering from hangovers and even Susan Paulin, upon whom, he realised with a jolt, he had come to rely on for an occasional smile, seemed unnaturally preoccupied.

The handset crackled and he picked it up. "Bridge – Aft. Tow's veered and secured, sir." Hobden's voice, level and efficient as usual, irritated him.

"About bloody time!" Naismith instantly regretted his demonstrably bad temper which only increased his irritation. He banged the engine controllers savagely to full speed and growled a course to the quarter-master. *Active* began to increase speed and the low line of the Essex coast lost its details and receded, only the blue stump of the Naze tower marking any point upon it.

He walked again out onto the bridge wing and stared astern at the tow. He could see the bluff red bow of the lightvessel and the chain pendant of the tow disappearing into the sea ahead of her, attached to *Active*'s heavy wire towing hawser. He saw it lift slightly as *Active* gathered way but it did not break the surface and the increased roll of water at the lightvessel's bow showed where the tow followed docilely.

Sobey came on the bridge.

"Have you had your dinner, Mr Sobey?"

"Yes, sir."

"Right, you may take the ship . . ." He handed the bridge over to the third officer and made his way down to the saloon. He realised that he was starving hungry. Apart from Sobey and the second engineer who were both on watch, all the other officers were assembled and at various stages of their meals. Chief Engineer Morrison was already leaning back, idly stirring a cup of coffee. Hobden had only just sat down and remained silent in mute protest at Naismith's earlier sharpness. Naismith dismissed the idea of a conciliatory remark, ordered soup and stared at the tablecloth.

The strange conviction that had overwhelmed him the previous evening following the television news had been compounded by an unsatisfactory phone call to his wife. He had come back to the ship profoundly depressed and stood looking at the photographs of his two children in his night cabin.

Ben, a disgracefully untidy teenage boy, his face pocked with the ravages of acne, easygoing but with the bustling energy of his mother when his interest was aroused. And Sarah, two years her brother's junior, on the brink of adolescence, her face still reminiscent of the child yet indicative of the growing woman. Her long lashes and large eyes promised a beauty greater than her mother's had been.

He had had a sudden nightmarish image of their faces puffed and yellow and purulent with lesions. He had wiped his hand roughly across his own mouth and found he was sweating. He did not dare to imagine what their loss in such circumstances would mean to him, and he had not shaken off that fear until the dawn was already lightening the eastern sky. When the steward called him he had woken tired, recalling the events of the previous evening and the lack of harmony with his wife. He had been unusually sharp-tempered during the operation of picking up the tow and realised belatedly, that his own preoccupations had affected his own efficiency.

". . . What did *you* think, sir?" asked Susan. "Did you see that news report last night?" He came out of his abstraction aware that Susan was addressing him.

"I'm sorry?" he said. "I was miles away."

"Did you see that film report from Costa Maya, sir?" she asked again.

"Er, yes I did. It was pretty appalling."

"Ms Paulin," said Mr Morrison, pronouncing the title in that mildly offensive bee's hum that it lent itself so irresistibly to, "has found an alternative cause to that of simple pollution."

"Well don't *you* think it's awful, Chief?" said Susan, the two points of colour appearing on her cheeks. Morrison shrugged and pulled the corners of his mouth down.

"What can one do about it? These things happen everyday somewhere in the world . . .

"Yes but that doesn't mean you should condone them."

"He doesn't condone them," Hobden replied on the chief engineer's behalf. Naismith took a sudden interest in Hobden's attitude towards Susan, wondering if Hobden the man or Hobden the mate had won. "What he says is true." Hobden swallowed his mouthful. "People like us are powerless to change

131

what is happening in some tin-pot banana republic in Central America." The mate, it appeared to Naismith, had come out on top. The steward placed a bowl of soup in front of him and he began to eat.

"Well that's a defeatist attitude," said Susan scornfully and Naismith saw Hobden flush. "If we objected a little more, perhaps some of these things would stop happening . . ."

"Come on, Susie," said Colin Mulliner, the third engineer, "it's all very well being altruistic but it isn't practical is it now? I mean what exactly could you do to stop these people dropping this stuff in Costa Maya, eh?" He patronised her with the jolly condescension of an older brother. Susan looked up, her eyes angry.

"Look, they probably get it from the Americans, that much was implied in last night's news. For a start one could mount a demonstration outside the American Embassy in London . . ."

"And cost the taxpayers a lot of money to keep it in order," put in Hobden. "You'd just be a menace, along with the rest of the wishy-washy liberal left."

"Oh come on Chas, that's a bit harsh," said Naismith as the steward cleared away the soup plate. "No, I agree with Susan's point of view. Nothing can possibly justify using weapons like this, particularly as the population this stuff was used on had elected a government which has been overthrown by the military."

"How do we know these reports are accurate?" said Hobden weakly. "I mean it wouldn't be difficult to fake something like this for political purposes . . ."

Naismith saw Susan's eyebrows arch and her eyes cast up. "Come on, Chas, you'll be telling me next that the Nazis didn't actually murder six million Jews

. . . No, it seems to me that the root of the problem is that the military can get away with their coup in the first place. Because the army in this country hasn't been a political force since Cromwell's time I think we underestimate what generals think about their role in other countries. The extreme measures they are using against the Costa Mayans would seem to indicate a conventional military weakness, which is hardly surprising in the circumstances."

Hobden sniffed. An intensely practical man with little interest in the outside world, he was contemptuous of semantics. Naismith turned on the chief engineer.

"As for you, Bill, I know bloody well that if someone was trying to drop this crap on your family you'd be pretty mad about it, wouldn't you?"

Morrison opened his mouth to speak but Susan was quick to seize the advantage Naismith's support gave her.

"It's contemptible to suggest that people shouldn't make their views known. You don't really believe that we should sit back and accept everything the powerful say and do, do you? I mean I can accept that you two," she nodded at Hobden and Morrison, "don't want to get *involved*, even that you can't be *bothered*, but surely you can't actually *believe* that it isn't your business."

"Look love," Morrison leaned forward irritably, "if it makes you any happier we all agree with you, but as there's sod all we can do about it we prefer to enjoy our dinner in peace. Okay?"

"Really, Chief," she snapped, "your complacency is beneath my contempt. If we weren't all so bloody complacent no one would dare to try and get away with these things!"

She got up from the table, her hazel eyes blazing

and her cheeks flushed with the anger boiling inside her. For the first time since the television news of the previous night he felt able to be amused. The chief's discomfiture was really quite funny.

"Well I'm damned," Morrison muttered.

"Cheeky young bitch," said Hobden revealingly.

But Naismith agreed with Susan. The difference between them was that she still believed there was a way out of these problems. He knew there was no longer sufficient time.

"Well, well," said Mulliner after a little. "Did I tell you about Susie and the condom?"

There was a spark of prurient interest round the table and choruses of "No," and "Go on then."

"Well it was while we were picking up the tow this morning. I was out on deck checking the port boat-hoisting winch and after I'd finished I wandered aft to see how they were doing . . ."

"I wondered what took you so bloody long," put in the chief, still testy after the rough ride given him by Susan and Naismith.

"I suppose you wanted to chat to a piece of skirt," said Hobden.

"Well don't be jealous, Chas," Mulliner said, grinning, "you've got to admit she's a tasty little dish which improves as the days pass. Anyway I was looking over the side and she pointed out a heap of rubbish floating out on the tide; and right in the middle was a used french letter . . ." A chuckle went round the table.

"Was she embarrassed?" asked Hobden.

Mulliner ignored the question. "'Look at that, Susie', I said, 'what's worse, that indestructible dreadnought polluting our coastline or an unwanted kid?'"

"What did she say to that?" asked Hobden again.

"She gave me one of her looks," replied Mulliner, "which meant I shouldn't be facetious but she hadn't worked out the answer to that one yet, so I suggested a solution."

"Oh yes," said the chief archly, "and what, may we ask, was that?"

"Ah, well, I suggested biodegradable condoms, french letters with built in obsolescence . . ."

The laughter ran round the table at the prospect of the discomfiture of the female by a bit of male innuendo.

"What was her reaction?" asked Naismith, amused in spite of himself.

"She trod on my foot, sir."

"Serve you right."

"Ah, but I was wearing my steel toe-capped boots," laughed Mulliner.

Susan had gone on deck and leaned on the rail to cool off. She knew she had exceeded the bounds of propriety as far as a second mate was concerned but she felt so strongly she did not care.

The seamen were washing down the decks and she was forced to give up her observation post as they came aft, chaffing and abusing each other with their hoses and brooms. She made to leave the deck when Davis accosted her.

"Excuse me, Miss."

"Yes?"

"Can I have a private word with you?"

She took him into her cabin. "What is it?"

"There's a rumour going round down below that that wrecked ship was carrying a hydrogen bomb, like. D'you know anything about it?"

She smiled and shook her head. "No." She knew what wild and fanciful stories could be whipped up by the ratings. "What on earth makes you think that?"

Davis shrugged. "They said you'd seen a submarine around the wreck, like, and then there was that navy ship. I just thought you might tell me if there was anything in it, you know?"

She shook her head again. "You're worried about your wife . . ." She was about to say "and baby" when she remembered what she had heard.

It was Davis's turn to nod. "What are you going to do about your wife? Can you get her out and over here?"

He looked at her, surprised she was interested. "I don't know. I'm trying to."

"You didn't see the news last night?"

He shook his head. "No. I went ashore, had a few bevvies . . . why?"

"They mentioned Costa Maya." She hesitated. "There's a lot of fighting going on, it seems, and a lot of refugees getting out of the country." She did not mention the nerve gas. It seemed unimportant now. "Do you think your wife might try and get out of the country?"

Davis looked at her sharply. "No, Miss. Juanita's lost the kid and may think I've left her too. She'll stay and fight them Fascist bastards."

He made to leave the cabin, then turned back. "Ta, Miss." He seemed about to say more, decided against it and was gone.

Frank Davis pulled on the donkey jacket and made his way onto the deck. The night was chilly, although the wind was light. *Active*, her speed reduced by the tow, was off the Varne, lifting easily to a low westerly swell. He relieved Ellice on the lookout forward and, hunching his shoulders, settled down, occasionally ringing the bell to indicate a ship crossing their track.

His mind drifted off into reverie. His plans were almost completed. As soon as his month of duty was up he would have enough money for an air fare to Mexico City. Once there he felt certain he would be able to contact Juanita somehow or other. Grief had coalesced into a cold sense of purpose. He had been played a poor trick by fate and the satisfaction he had derived from hitting Harris had awoken in him the idea of influencing events himself. He was sick of being a victim of circumstance.

So he kept his lookout, and made his plans, and bided his time.

Naismith ruminated unhappily in his cabin, the light relief afforded him in the saloon long forgotten. He had been up and down to the bridge all day, ostensibly because of the tow, but in fact he had scarcely given it a thought since they had cleared the coast. It seemed that since the *Active* had been despatched to the wreck of the *Wallenstein* the tranquillity of his life had been perpetually disturbed. But no, that was not true, the business of the *Wallenstein* and her odious cargo seemed merely to have highlighted the unhappiness of his marriage. He had worked out the connection in his own mind, but the one seemed to bring the other to a crisis.

After the depressing and terrible realisation that the television news of the previous evening had brought him, he had gone ashore to telephone his wife. It had been a less than satisfactory conversation, stale with old arguments and terminated abruptly when he ran out of money.

Wendy belied her little-girl name. Immensely practical, she had shouldered the burden of bringing up two children with the same energy she had displayed as a nurse. As a mother she was quite beyond reproach and somehow his own dissatisfaction seemed unreasonable when faced with her virtues. But her very efficiency sometimes made him a stranger in his own home. She was intolerant of his weariness when he went on leave while he, released from the tensions of the ship, gave way to ill-tempered sallies that poisoned the atmosphere from the start. He could sense the relief when he began to gather his kit together again, and himself felt, albeit unwillingly, a great sense of liberation as the front door closed behind him. He tried to tell himself it was the price he paid for being a seaman, that Wendy paid for marrying one, but it was cold comfort. He was passionately fond of his children who in turn were well aware of the differences between their parents. It appeared to Naismith in his depression that his failure as a husband seemed to reflect something of the accelerating decay that filled the world. There was nothing to prevent him and his family being supremely happy; except some built-in defect that prevented that felicitous state.

Naismith sighed, recollecting Wendy's final words, uttered with that forthright tactlessness that pained him so much. He found himself wishing that Susan was right and that there was something he could do to change the condition of the world. He remembered the dolphins and tried to see their reappearance as a sign that all might not yet be too late. But he knew that to be mere foolish wishful thinking. He saw *Harwich* in his mind's eye, that superb artefact devised by man.

He saw her captain, an intelligent man engaged in activities of a morally dubious nature. He saw the dead body of the diver as *prima facie* evidence that those drums were lethal; he saw Davis and that fortuitous link with Costa Maya. And that woman and child, the defiled image of the Christian message.

The weather was kind to them. The end of September approached and there was no sign of the onset of the seasonal gales the old-timers still called "the equinoctials". The new lightvessel was laid on her station and the moorings inspected by Scranton and Walker while the rendezvous with another BNAS ship, the *Able*, which arrived to tow the old lightvessel off station to her dry-docking in Southampton, passed off without incident.

Only Hobden seemed unhappy about things. There had been a minor hitch in the operation of slipping the tow and he made it clear to Susan Paulin that he held her responsible. For her own part Susan had acknowledged her error. As the officer in charge of the after gang she must be held accountable and in matters of seamanship Hobden was never in the wrong.

"I'm sorry," she said when he had finished his lecture.

"Well it was a bloody cock-up."

"Look, I've said I'm sorry. It was only a fouled line and we had it cleared in no time at all . . ."

"Listen, Miss," Hobden said with a sudden vehemence, "I'll tolerate your ideas in the saloon, but out on deck it goes *my* way, right? So far you've been lucky. Everybody's made allowances for you . . ."

"What d'you mean?" she said suddenly, drawing herself up.

"I mean there are plenty of people on board who

resent your being here. You're stopping a man getting a wage and getting away with bloody murder because you're a woman." He paused, then added as she began to reply, "And you damn well know it."

"That's very unfair. What on earth have I done?"

"All this bloody nonsense about pollution has gone too far. The bosun tells me, you stopped him dumping rubbish overboard yesterday; you attack the chief engineer at the table and carry on as if you're the one who says what goes round here."

"The bosun was chucking oily cotton waste and old paint tins over the side. There was some waste oil too. You know that is illegal. Anyway these things *are* important . . ."

"The only thing that's important is that you do what you're told, Miss, like any other second mate. Just because you've been sucking up to the Old Man doesn't mean you can bugger around on deck. That's my business and don't you damned well forget it!"

Susan closed her open mouth and gave up. It was futile to argue against Hobden. Ships, like small towns, were prone to storms in teacups. She should not be surprised at the resentment. It had had to come from someone and, now that she considered the matter, it was bound to be Hobden. She had felt a curious threat from him from the beginning. He was a bachelor and so narrow-minded that it made one embarrassed. She walked out of the wardroom.

Once in her cabin she drowned her angry frustration in washing out a few items of underwear. Why was it men acquiesced to the status quo with such terrifying indifference? Was it really because it was a world of *their* making?

She could not believe that, it was too simplistic a view. Peter was not like that. Neither was the captain, once one scraped aside the facade he was at such pains to maintain. She remembered Hobden's accusation of her over-familiarity with Captain Naismith and found it made her more angry than his other, ignorant accusations. She sniffed and wiped her nose as she bent over the cabin wash-basin. A smudge of lather hung on her cheek. She swore and pulled the plug, rinsing her clothes and wiping her face.

Active rolled slightly as, on the bridge, Sobey altered course. Her cabin door swung open.

"Hi!" She looked up. Walker, the assistant diver, leaned in the doorway. His checked shirt was open to the waist and a large gold ingot gleamed on the hairy expanse of his exposed chest.

"What do you want?" She was still bent over the washbasin, rinsing her underwear for the second time. Her hair was slightly dishevelled and she had taken off her pullover. Her blouse was thin cotton and open at the neck. She already knew what he wanted. The winks and suggestive clucks he had subjected her to when he had first come aboard had led her to suppose that she was expected to throw herself at his feet.

"I, er, heard you were in some kind of, er, trouble . . ." He moved inside the cabin a step as she tossed the hair out of her eyes, pulled the plug a second time and began to wring out the tights and briefs. "I thought you might want someone to talk it through with." The mid-Atlantic accent and the affected concern went with the macho image and she looked at him for a moment in stunned disbelief. He took the stare for interest and began to close the door.

"Are you real?" she asked scornfully. "And leave that door alone!"

"Sure, baby." He was smiling and shrugged in a studied, half-familiar way. She took a step towards him, furious. He was still smiling and one hand was raised and rested on her shoulder.

"I don't believe this. Look will you take your hands off and get out!" Her voice was low in an effort at self-control.

"I realise you're hung up, baby. Sometimes a man can make you hang loose . . ." The voice was smooth, unbelievably self-assured. His other hand came up and covered her breast.

"I need a man like a fish needs a bicycle . . ." She pushed him hard in the chest and he staggered back.

"Hey, baby, what did I do . . .?"

"Get out!" Her voice was raised now and Walker suddenly took alarm. Her eyes were blazing and it dawned on him that his charisma had failed.

"Get out!"

He retreated disbelievingly and Susan leaned back on the bunk, trembling and with her face in her hands.

Naismith heard the row between Hobden and Susan. He did not interfere. Susan looked rather chastened that afternoon as they completed the last task of the day, but she had been a model of efficiency as they had serviced the Blanchard buoy off Sark. Darkness had already fallen as they altered course to the north-west and St Peter Port Roads.

"Right," he said entering the wheelhouse from the wing, "Lower Heads buoy in the morning and then, er . . ." His orders gave him wide latitude and he was aware of wavering. He felt he should return to the wreck of the *Wallenstein*, but to what purpose?

He had asked himself that question a hundred times and a hundred times the same answer came back to him: to find that missing drum.

He had a hunch that the Royal Navy had failed to locate it, that it was still on the seabed, somewhere near the *Wallenstein*. But one lousy forty-gallon drum at the bottom of the English Channel was less conspicuous than the proverbial needle in a haystack.

Chapter Eleven

Naismith woke with a start, his heart hammering and a dreadful fear in possession of his wits. He tried to throw off the shadow of the nightmare and settle himself to sleep again but that proved impossible. The short stupor into which he had fallen had taken the edge off his tiredness, for his was no real physical exhaustion and his brain was now wide awake, chiding him from sleep like some persistent internal alarm. He sighed, rolled on his back and stared at the pale rectangle of the cabin deckhead above him. The horror still clung to him, a strange primaeval fear that at this lonely hour induced the very real sensation of terror.

His heart pounded from the dream-induced adrenalin that had poured unused into his blood. He tried to edit the tangle of his thoughts in an oddly pedantic way, offering each up to his conscious mind to see if they attracted any reaction.

The ship? No, *Active* was safely anchored and the reassuring tread of the watch overhead suppressed anxiety on that score. Home? His wife? No, there was no more than a constant feeling of familiar unease in that direction, a vague feeling of failure. His children? A faint stirring, of being on the right track, filled him and the speed of his thoughts quickened . . .

The woman, the hideously maimed child and the drums . . .

He sat up, realising that he could prevaricate no longer. Swinging his legs over the edge of the bunk he stared into the near darkness. He had known for a long time that he would have to go back, to bend his orders if necessary. He felt it was his duty to return to the wreck of the *Wallenstein*. Not his duty to BNAS but an obligation to his children and to that hopeless scrap of humanity that the wonders of television had thrust into his life. He hoped too that he might achieve something, something that would vindicate him as a husband and father, something that would counteract the evil folly of the mutant species he saw man as. Call it fate, providence, predestination, even God, but Naismith did not doubt now that the strands of the mystery had been laid in his lap for a purpose.

He got up and padded naked into his bathroom to relieve himself. Then he draped a towel round himself and went through into his day cabin. Switching on the desk light he sat down and drew a sheet of paper towards him. Picking up a ballpoint pen he began to write. After about half an hour he began drawing a series of diagrams, occasionally scribbling over one and doing it again.

He had been thus occupied for nearly an hour when he became aware of subdued but angry words in the alleyway. He stopped what he was doing and listened. The voices came to him through the open but curtained door. There was no mistaking the urgent fury of one of the voices. Nor its sex.

"No! Please go away!"

"Hey, baby, c'm'on now . . ."

"You bastard . . ."

Naismith flung the curtain aside and stepped out

into the alleyway. At the after end of the officers' accommodation Walker, dressed only in jeans, was pushing his way into Susan's cabin. Naismith could see only her hand and arm as he advanced angrily. He bit off the bellow that mounted to his lips. He could spare Susan that embarrassment. Naismith's sense of outrage and authority made him forget the simple fact that a fit young man like Walker could make mincemeat of him. The diver was unaware of his approach and Naismith had spun him round, out of the cabin doorway, before Walker knew what had happened. The diver fell back a pace and Naismith smelt the reek of whisky on his breath.

"What the hell . . .?"

"Get to bed at once," he snapped.

Walker recovered himself, frowning as he gathered his wits and hunched his shoulders.

"Get to your cabin before I call the watch and have you restrained."

Walker looked at the captain and at the closing door of Susan's cabin.

"Oh, I get the scene. Trespassing on the Old Man's perks am I . . .?" Naismith's fist drove into the diver's gut and Walker staggered backwards.

"You bastard!" he hissed, partially winded. Naismith stepped forward and Walker, holding his stomach, fell back, leaning on the alleyway door. He straightened to take a swing at Naismith.

"Get out!" hissed Naismith. The unlatched, heavy teak door swung open under Walker's weight. The high sea-step caught his calves and he overbalanced. He went over onto the deck on his back with a bone-jarring thud. Naismith grabbed both heels and threw his legs after him and pulled the door to. He shot the bolt. It had all taken less than a minute.

147

He knocked on Susan's door. "Are you all right?" he asked in a low voice.

The door opened slightly and her pale face appeared.

"Are you all right?" he repeated. She nodded. "Sure?"

"Yes, sir."

"Come along to my cabin and have a shot of something."

"No, I'd rather not."

"Come on . . . I'd better make that an order, eh? You'll sleep better for it."

He returned to his cabin, slipped through to the night cabin and pulled on a pair of trousers. He reappeared in the dayroom as she came haltingly through the doorway. She wore a plain blue dressing gown and her hands were shaking. Despite her protests she looked as though she needed a drink. He flipped open the locker and brought out the Martel cognac. Pouring out a peg for her he helped himself to a whisky.

She sat on the edge of the settee and he squatted on the corner of the desk. He ran his fingers through his uncombed hair. "Are you sure you're quite all right, Susan?"

She managed a smile. "Yes, sir. I'm really quite all right, honestly."

"Has that happened to you before?"

She nodded. "Once." She clearly did not want to enlarge.

"Has Walker bothered you before?"

She shrugged. "Well, one or two of them think it's big to make the occasional provocative remark. Most of the time it's just a joke . . . but, er," she shook her head and smiled again, "but he was unbelievable . . . he really convinced himself he was really something . . ."

"He made you a proposition, eh?"

"Leave it, sir. I don't want to make a fuss and I don't suppose he'll do it again."

"No." Naismith paused. He could see her point. She had made a great success as the first female officer in BNAS and earned a measure of respect from the ship's company. A "fuss" would attract attention, the very thing she wished to avoid.

"Okay. But it won't hurt to have a word with Walker in the morning, I won't make it official."

"Thank you, sir." She finished the glass and he reached for the bottle. "No, no more . . ."

"Just the other half . . ." He slopped the brandy into the glass. "Besides, there's something I want to ask you. Oh, it's nothing about what has just happened."

He looked at her. It was a cruel abuse of power to keep her up like this, but he needed a confidante if he was going to achieve anything and Susan had declared herself the champion of the ocean. Besides, he might have trouble persuading Scranton to dive. He reckoned Susan would be better able to convince the diver than himself. And further, the project would take her mind off the events of the last few minutes.

"What is it then, sir?" She looked tired now.

"It's directly related to your interest in pollution, Susan." He saw a look of faint exasperation cross her face. "It's important and there *is* something you can do about it."

She frowned uncertainly.

"It's to do with the wreck of the *Wallenstein*."

"I don't understand."

"The *Wallenstein* sailed from Hamburg with a cargo

which included a stow of drums on deck labelled 'Dry- Cleaning Fluid' and consigned to Santa Maria de los Mayas, the capital of Costa Maya where, as you know, there is a guerilla war going on. As you also know from the television, the military are using nerve gas against the population . . . spraying it from aircraft, I suppose, and . . ."

"Those drums," she said excitedly.

"Contained the highly concentrated nerve gas agent."

"My God!"

"I suppose having Davis on board made me feel we had some personal involvement, particularly when I began to realise exactly what was going on." He saw a frown cross her face. "Listen, I'll explain."

"It was a perfectly routine matter until the super-intendent ordered me not to dive. By then it was too late. I suppose someone who knew about *Wallenstein*'s cargo got wind of her wreck and what was going on. They wanted us out of it PDQ, even at the risk of someone fouling those ropes . . ."

"That means somebody in the UK knew about the nerve agent!"

"Exactly. Which indicates it may have come from Germany. You see the wreck details are passed from BNAS to the Hydrographic Department of the Admiralty. No doubt their content may be scrutinised by other departments of the navy, intelligence for instance, who might have been aware of *Wallenstein*'s cargo and her destination. Anyway, to go on . . .

"Scranton didn't tell me at the time because he was pretty frightened, but when he went down he came across the body of a diver, a British Naval Diver whose hands were eaten away and whose face registered some kind of poisoning. One drum had been damaged and the poor devil must have swum right into a leak of the stuff."

Susan sat up, completely attentive. "That submarine I had on the sonar!"

"That's right. She put the divers onto the wreck. Scranton reckons two, one returned to report, leaving the body of his mate. I expect he knew what had happened. Anyway, we didn't know any of this and after laying the buoy went off to replenish the Buccabu lighthouse. The next thing I heard was that I was to remove the buoy. Meanwhile the authorities knew the stuff had to be got up. I suppose as much to prevent anybody else getting hold of it and making a great deal of propaganda mileage out of it . . ."

"My God, yes! If the Russians or the Green parties knew this stuff came from Germany it would really put the cat among the pigeons . . ."

"Well it may *not* be from a military dump, of course. German industrialists have been known to produce some pretty lethal chemicals in their time, but of course anyone interested in a propaganda coup needn't worry about such niceties. It's a gift to them: consignment of nerve gas agent from Germany in a flag-of-convenience ship bound for Santa Maria for use by an extremely right-wing government against a peasant population. A government moreover which usurped power from the democratically elected administration." He paused and reflected for a moment. "But I think that the swift intervention of the Royal Navy, as an arm of the NATO alliance, argues that the stuff probably comes from a military dump of some sort; German, American, perhaps, or even, God help us, British." He sighed. "You know it occurred to me that a few atomised clouds of this stuff might be easier and cheaper to deliver than Cruise,

Pershings and SS 20s. And if one side's got the stuff, it's odds-on that the other has too."

"There are reports about it being used in Afghanistan." She paused. "Did you say the drums on board *Harwich* were marked 'Dry-Cleaning Fluid'?"

"Yes . . . you think that argues that they came from a British source?"

She nodded. "Yes."

"Hmmm. It's a possibility, but the title is clearly a bluff. It's better to mark them in the international language of the sea so that the bluff is better understood by more people, including any interpreters of photographs, so the fact that they are marked in English is not necessarily conclusive. But I agree it's suspicious. I reckon the stuff is absolutely lethal in very small doses and they gave the tide time to disperse the leak. They may have of course wanted the body of the submarine's diver . . ." Susan pulled a face. "Yes, it isn't a very pleasant little story is it?" Naismith went on. "If they did have any trouble, *Harwich* had a helicopter flight deck for medical evacuation; she was big enough to deter any cloak and dagger behaviour by interested Eastern Bloc trawlers, with which the western approaches crawl at this time of the year with the mackerel running . . ."

"And wasn't too conspicuous in the area either. Yes I see. If this nerve agent is so lethal they wouldn't want any more leaks either, particularly if it might poison fish about to be caught by Polish, Rumanian or Russian trawlers . . ."

"Exactly."

They both fell silent. The scenario they had outlined seemed too fantastic, too much like a James Bond screenplay to be truly credible. It was two in the morning, an hour when such fancies can grip a tired imagination and fill it with hideous images. Naismith poured himself another whisky but Susan declined a further brandy.

"No thank you, sir." She paused, then added, "What I don't understand is how this affects us. Now, I mean. Since the *Harwich* recovered all the drums . . ."

"Ah, but I don't think she did. When I went aboard her captain as good as told me that and I have a hunch that at least one drum is still on the seabed."

"You think they've left a drum there?"

He nodded. "My guess is that they have cut their losses. The pollution caused by one drum they will consider negligible," he held up his hand to silence her protest that no pollution was negligible," and that if they can't find it, then neither can anyone else. I think that they have abandoned the search because to carry it on any longer might attract the wrong sort of attention . . ."

"From the mackerel fishermen?"

"Yes. You see it stands to reason that the drum, or drums, that are missing are not close to the wreck, or *Harwich*'s divers would have found them. *Harwich* wasn't supposed to be on scene when we arrived to remove the buoy. She had been delayed in looking for the missing drum. Her captain was perturbed that we'd put a diver on the wreck, that's how I found out they hadn't succeeded in their mission, at least not properly."

"And what d'you intend to do about it, sir?" She looked up at him with troubled eyes.

"Get that drum up."

Susan sat stunned. She could not believe Naismith was serious. Apart from the apparent impossibility of the task it was such an uncharacteristic thing to do. It would be a gross breach of orders. Captain Naismith's *modus operandi* was one of caution in all things. He was not a man to take chances and for all her horror of the filthy stuff that lay on the floor of the Channel, for all her revulsion at the use of such material against women and children, she could not believe that the dishevelled figure toying with the remains of his third whisky was the kind of man to take the offensive. He must have divined something of her thoughts for he said in a low, confidential voice, "Well Susan, you've been preaching for long enough. Are you with me or not? Because I need someone in whom I can confide if we are to get this thing up. Two brains are better than one at this sort of thing . . ."

She avoided a direct answer. "If the navy didn't get it, how do you propose to find it?"

He smiled. "Look . . ." He turned round and sat at his desk, pulling up the coffee table for her to perch on. He spread out a series of drawings.

"The *Cutty Sark* gave me the clue."

"The tea-clipper?" she asked in astonishment, wondering whether Naismith might have taken leave of his senses.

"Yes. I'll show you. This is a stow of drums on deck, hard up against the outboard bulwarks, right? It's lashed by wire set tight by bottle screws, the whole thing set up using the bulwark stays. The stow is therefore tensioned outboard, against the restraint of the bulwarks. Okay?"

"Yes, so far."

"Good. Take away the bulwark and ripple the deck beneath and some of the drums will fall outboard . . ."

"Onto the bow of the colliding vessel . . ."

"Right, particularly when you know the *Calliope* was a coaster, smaller than the *Wallenstein* and consequently lower in the water. Now look, Scranton seemed to think that the main gash was opened up by *Calliope*'s anchor. Both ships were going ahead at the time of the collision and *Calliope* drove into *Wallenstein* sufficiently far to open a 'V' to her water line and start her listing as the water rushed in. At that point one, maybe two, drums landed on *Calliope*'s bow. *Wallenstein*'s the bigger ship and drags *Calliope* along. Both, or either, may be going astern, it doesn't matter, what matters is that *Calliope*'s anchor rips open a hole large enough to seriously damage *Wallenstein*'s hull in two holds. She's listing and the list is increasing. Now what are you told if you collide and you have hit another ship's side?"

"Go ahead and fill the hole."

"That's fine in theory and if both ships are almost stationary. But if one is dragging the other along with her, there's a screech of metal and people panic. Almost anything can happen. *Calliope* may have gone ahead again, perhaps to fill the hole, perhaps to disentangle her anchor, it doesn't matter. What matters is she put another hole in *Wallenstein* in way of the engine room. *Wallenstein* hadn't a chance, filled and sank. All the time this was going on, *Wallenstein* was shedding drums in a line along her last few cables of track. I doubt the gap in her bulwarks was very big bearing in mind the size of *Calliope* and the fact that some drums were still on board when the RN diver arrived, one of which had been trapped and punctured by the bulwark plating folding back."

"How did you know what size the *Calliope* was?"

"There was a picture of her in Lloyd's in Captain Campbell's office. I hadn't realised what I was looking at until later. I was half-listening to Campbell's conversation with the Chief Executive, since it concerned me."

"So the navy worked along the line of drums . . ."

"Missing the one on *Calliope*'s bow."

"But *Calliope* went to Cherbourg. If you're right then the drum was sitting on her fo'c's'le head. And her crew would have known all about it."

"That's what stumped me until I remembered about the *Cutty Sark*." He smiled at her confused expression. "You see I reckoned the crew of the *Wallenstein* didn't know what was in the drums. Maybe the master did but I doubt it. He'd take the cargo-manifest at face value. So would the crew of *Calliope*. I expect the authorities, considering in their usual manner that the merchant seamen of any nation are not far above the level of common swine, have ruled out the possibility of any security leak there, particularly as they landed in France . . ."

"And St Peter Port, sir," she reminded him.

He shrugged. "Okay, but that doesn't materially alter the case."

"Go on. About the *Cutty Sark*."

"Right. It's pretty certain *Calliope* arrived in Cherbourg without any *incriminating* drums on her deck. I remembered a story about the carpenter of the *Cutty Sark*. He was serving in another ship and this second ship was anchored in the Downs in a gale from the west, waiting for a favourable wind down Channel. Among the other vessels there was his favourite, the *Cutty Sark*. Right? Well the night came on and it was blowing hard and some ships began to drag. One of them was the *Cutty Sark* and she dragged her anchor right down onto this other ship with her former chippy in her. The two ships got foul and there was a lot of crunching and smashing of gear. Of course the carpenter was ordered forward and the first thing he sees as the colliding ship tears free is the nameboard from the *Cutty Sark*. So, seeing how he remembers the old ship with affection, he picks it up and chucks it over the side."

She looked at him blankly.

"He threw away the incriminating evidence. If the *Calliope*'s crew ran forward to look at the damage might they not have regarded the drum as similarly incriminating, damaging to their own interests?"

She imagined the bang as the two ships struck, their respective angles as reconstructed by Naismith, the backing off and grinding of the two hulls as they continued their two movements relative to each other. There would have been a sudden emergence of their frightened crews, a lot of shouting and running forward on the little *Calliope* to examine the extent of the damage. A running aft to shout up at the wheelhouse. *Calliope*'s master in an agony of indecision over what to do, suddenly confronted with this appalling disaster in the middle of the night. She tried to put herself in the position of the master of *Calliope*, a commercial shipmaster with a cargo to run, an owner to satisfy in a murderously competitive world and a wife waiting near the Piraeus. She knew the man might have been feeling as guilty as hell, even turned in, despite the fog, and probably going at full speed. It was almost certain that he would have shouted to any query from forward that the drum should be ditched.

"But that would mean the drum was tossed over while *Calliope* was quite close to *Wallenstein*, and therefore ought to have been found by the navy."

"Not necessarily. Look." He bent again over his sketches. "If you assume that the master of *Calliope* was asleep and that she was going full speed, neither of which are impossible. Let's say that he is guilty and his conscience is troubling him when he takes over from whoever had the bridge, okay? It's dense fog and he goes through the various manoeuvres that we've talked about which finally result in him backing off the *Wallenstein* while she lists over and sinks. Now, the master of the *Calliope* is not a naval-trained automaton, he's a frightened and guilty Greek shipmaster whose first thought is for his livelihood so he checks out his ship and finds that the damage to her isn't catastrophic. This takes some time. *Calliope* drifts in the tide. Perhaps he leaves the bridge to check things himself. By this time *Wallenstein* is at best a glow of light in the fog, may have been plunged into darkness due to water entering her engine room, or may already have sunk. By the time our friend recollects his obligations to the other ship under International Law, they are some distance apart and are probably completely out of touch. *Wallenstein*'s master will have been jamming all radio frequencies with Mayday calls but *Calliope*, a small coaster with minimal crew, has simply not been paying attention. Now I've worked out what I reckon happened when the *Calliope* eventually got under way and located the wreckage and I reckon that the *Calliope*'s captain shouted for that drum to be tossed overboard about here, shortly after he got his ship underway again, and if he turned up into the tide, giving him a turning circle of say two cables, I'd say that a positive order like that would be given in the period of reaction, after he'd come out of the first shock and was beginning to get a grip. He probably began to bawl and shout at his second mate, or whoever had the watch when the collision occurred." He stopped at last, his finger pointing to a pencilled "X" on his drawing.

"You base that last assumption on experience, do you, sir?" she asked smiling. He nodded.

"'Fraid so," he smiled ruefully back at her.

She looked again at the sketch. "I think you're right."

"Then you'll help me get this drum up, no matter what the consequences?"

"I don't think I like to think too much about them, sir . . ."

"No, perhaps not . . . Still the cause is worthwhile, wouldn't you say?"

"Oh yes. Yes," she added firmly, "the cause is worthwhile, whether it's a matter of pollution or stopping that business in Costa Maya."

Naismith nodded. "Okay, so we go and get the drum. The problem is what do we do when we've got it? Do we publicise our find or quietly hand it over to the navy and hope for a pat on the head?"

Susan looked at him sharply. "That would be dishonest, sir! It wouldn't stop the use of the stuff in Costa Maya or anywhere else for that matter. Whoever is behind this thing should have thought about playing into the hands of whoever they're afraid of before they shipped the stuff out of Europe. It strikes me as significant that if the television reports are correct and the United States *are* supplying this horrible regime they have to ship it out of *European* stockpiles."

"That hadn't occurred to me." He paused for a last-ditch struggle with his acquiescence to authority. "Okay, so we go for publicity . . ."

"Then that's no problem!" said Susan standing up, her eyes bright with excitement. "I've a friend who's an investigative marine journalist. He's got a lot of contacts, and I shouldn't be surprised if we can't get something from him. If we can get in touch . . ." She nodded at the Satcomm telephone that sat on Naismith's desk.

"At three-thirty in the morning?" Naismith remembered Susan's friend Peter.

"Good investigative journalists, like good shipmasters, sleep lightly."

"Okay." Quick, discreet and direct, the Satellite Communications telephone seemed ideal for such unorthodox use. "D'you know his number?"

"Oh yes," she said with just hint enough to explain something of her private life.

She picked up the telephone and keyed in the digits. There was a long pause.

"Peter? Hullo, darling . . . yes, it's me. Sorry to wake you but I've got a story for you . . ." She paused and put her hand over the mouthpiece. Turning to Naismith she smiled. "It never fails to get his attention." She removed her hand. "Ready? Right, here goes. The Liberian cargo ship *Wallenstein* . . . yes the one sunk by *Calliope* . . . okay, you know, well listen. Captain Naismith and I have very good reason to believe that she was carrying drums of some highly concentrated form of poison, probably a nerve gas agent. We think that while we were wreck-marking, a submarine came close and put a diving team on the location of the wreck. When our own diver went down he located the body of a diver . . . eh? No, British . . . yes, standard RN gear . . . okay? Right, well we were warned off the wreck and later told to go back and take off the buoy we'd put on it. We found a destroyer, the *Harwich*, sitting on top of it. She had a diving team down to locate the wreck and the navy were

160

very touchy about our people taking photographs. Captain Naismith, my Captain, was summoned on board and came away with the impression that the navy were still looking for something despite the fact that they had a stow of drums on deck all marked as Dry-Cleaning Fluid . . . what? Er, wait." She turned to Naismith. "What was her captain's name?"

"Troughton."

"Troughton," she continued into the telephone. "The thing that really got us onto this thing was the destination of the *Wallenstein*. It's Santa Maria de los Mayas, yes, yes, the capital . . . we know . . . and there was a tele-report about nerve gas . . . yes, you saw it too . . . Well we think there's a connection . . ." She took her mouth away from the phone and said to Naismith: "He's onto it already, sir . . ." Her eyes shone and she tossed her hair as she replaced the phone to her ear.

"Listen, Peter, d'you think you can get any information . . . what?" She sounded surprised and was silent for some time. At last she said, "My God! Well, look . . . yes, we've thought about all the implications . . . yes, yes, that too. Look Peter, you know how I feel about this sort of thing and Captain Naismith says that if there's a chance of stopping the business, he thinks he knows where the missing drum is. There's a possibility we could get it . . . yes . . . can you phone us back via satellite and the Goonhilly station at, say one a.m. tomorrow . . ." She passed the ship's number, blew a kiss and hung up. "Phew!"

"You said he's already onto it?"

"Yes, sir. Apparently there's a story about two fishermen in St Peter Port hospital after handling dead fish somewhere near the Hurd Deep."

Naismith's eyes widened. "Then the barrel that

leaked all over the diver had other effects. Jesus, the stuff must be horribly potent."

Susan nodded. "Peter says that there is quite a story about that alone, what we've given him is sensational."

"I'll bet," said Naismith thoughtfully, and then he remembered something else. "Did you say two fishermen?" She nodded. "I'll bet that's the *Three Brothers*!"

"Two . . ."

"No, no, the fishing boat that advised us he could smell oil; you weren't on the bridge. He said one of his crew wasn't feeling well. Did your friend say whether they were alive or what?"

She shook her head again. "Didn't say."

"This friend of yours, you called him a marine reporter. What the hell's that?"

"He specialises in marine matters. I told you. He's a former merchant navy officer so his facts will be checked and his technical details correct."

"That'll make a change then," Naismith smiled. He took a deep breath, then said with sudden passion, "Christ, Susan, you realise there's no turning back now! We've burned our boats well and truly!"

"Yes," she said smiling at him, all thoughts of the unpleasant intrusion earlier banished from her mind. "Yes, but what else could we do?" She added quietly, "it's so important to be true to ourselves."

Naismith raised a cynical eyebrow. Put in that direct way their action seemed to have that quality of truth made ridiculous by cliché. He nodded. "Yes, and now you must be off to bed." He was quite unprepared for the quick peck on the cheek that she gave him.

"Remember the dolphins," she said and was gone.

Naismith slipped his trousers off. He thought once

more of the reasons for his action. Perhaps there was, after all, a sense of obligation to his wife. He thought of Davis and his distant wife Juanita, and the power of Susan's passion. "Women," he muttered to himself as he flung his trousers onto the bedside chair, but he was smiling as he composed himself for sleep.

Chapter Twelve

Charles Hobden could not sleep either. The uncharacteristic wakefulness that made him toss and turn uncomfortably in the narrow bunk was the result of his argument in the wardroom with Susan Paulin. Despite having had the last word he felt very unsettled by the whole experience. At first he thought it was due to the threat she seemed to pose to the unassailable position enjoyed by himself for so many years as *Active*'s chief mate, *the* mate, a part of the ship as much as her foremast or funnel. He was aware of a strong resentment towards a girl foisted upon him as a second mate because of some lunatic legislation by a bunch of limp-wristed politicians who pursued their doctrinaire goals without any real thought as to the consequences. Somehow her presence diminished his own achievement. It was bad enough being passed over by a poodle-faking ex-liner man like Naismith, but at least Hobden's exacting judgement could not fault the captain's ability. His bitter reflections on the apparent policy of BNAS to promote well-spoken officers rather than humbler worthies like himself was an oft-considered grievance. But it was set at nothing beside the contemplation of being placed on an unequal footing with the likes of Ms Bloody Paulin.

But his sleeplessness was not due solely to the

seminal feeling that women aboard ship were as improper as striptease artistes in the Vatican. What lay beneath the distress of Charles Hobden was the growing realisation that Susan Paulin had affected them all. There was no doubt that Naismith felt attracted to his new second mate, Hobden was sure of that, and he himself had to admit that he felt a pang of jealousy. It was not a new sensation. Jealousy of Naismith extended beyond the purely professional aspects of their relationships. He had known Wendy Naismith for as many years as he had served with her husband and had always admired her. A handsome, capable woman, she had seemed an ideal, married, of course, to a man destined to succeed and who, Hobden knew, did not fully appreciate her. He remembered a Christmas party when Colin Mulliner, the ship's Lothario, had arrived with a flashy girl who promptly got horribly drunk and made a scene which culminated in her throwing up all over the carpet in Mulliner's cabin.

Wendy had soothed the girl, compelled Mulliner to get her ashore and helped clean up. "I don't think your husband would approve, if he knew about this," he had said as they laboured to clean the mess off the deck. They both squatted and in her party dress Wendy's proximity only added to the effects of the rum he had been drinking. Aware of her body crouched a foot from his own he had kissed her cheek.

She had stopped wielding the clout and looked at him. For a second he thought she might allow him to go further, then she shook her head. "He wouldn't approve of that either, Chas . . ." But she had smiled at him and there had been an intimacy between them ever since.

Hobden had never been a promiscuous man. Like many seamen he had purchased his earliest pleasures, but these had been from need, not incontinence. The steadiness of his nature had dominated his sexual relationships as much as his single-minded pursuit of his professional advancement. It therefore came to him as a shock to realise why he could not sleep.

The row he had had with Susan had not unsettled him because of any real threat to himself, or to his position on board *Active*. What bothered him was the fact that he realised he had enjoyed it, enjoyed the feeling of dominating the girl. And with this came the full acknowledgement to himself that he was powerfully sexually attracted to her, that her constant appearance was a continual torment to him. It therefore came as a shock to him to find his whole being rocked by irresistible concupiscence. But it was sadly clear that Susan did not find him in the least appealing. Her contempt for his attitudes clearly admitted no affection for his person.

Hobden flung his bedclothes aside and swung his powerful legs over the edge of the bunk. He strode across the cabin and opened the port to get some air. The sight of Walker vomitting over the deck-planking recalled Hobden to his duty. Pulling on a pair of trousers he stepped into the alleyway and out on deck.

"What the hell d'you think you're doing, my lad?"

Walker looked up. The blow on the back of his head as he had hit the deck outside the port alleyway door had laid him out cold for some time, assisted as it was by a quantity of whisky. When he had come to he had been bewildered by his exposed surroundings and begun a slow, uncertain journey to his cabin. A few moments on his feet and a staggering descent to the upper deck had laid him out again for some time. His head was spinning from the whisky and his gut beginning a series of contractions initiated by both the Scotch and the violence of Naismith's assault. After a while he got to his feet again and made for the lighted door of the athwartships alleyway that led below. Once over the sea-step he felt the first heave of his abused stomach and staggered forward, stumbling through the athwartships alleyway, crashing over the starboard sea-step in a vain attempt to reach the ship's side. He fell full length on the starboard upper deck, outside Hobden's cabin and began a series of violent eructations that twisted him as though in a fit. Now he looked up at the mate.

Hobden's beard made a curious impression on Walker's fuddled brain and the deck lights shone round the mate's ruffled hair like a halo, so that Walker, feeling like death, thought he might be in the presence of his maker. This impression was heightened for a moment as he felt himself lifted under the armpits. He let his head loll back and a few seconds later he felt a strange cold begin to seep through him.

"There my lad. That'll sober you up. And in the morning you can scrub the bloody deck." Hobden left the fire hydrant playing over the now stirring body and straightened up. He felt better. For a moment his thoughts had not been dominated by images of Susan's nubile figure and he had been master of a familiar situation.

Walker made pathetic movements away from the stream of cold sea water and uttered what Hobden took to be excuses.

"But I only wanted to kiss her . . ."

Hobden made out the slurred words and their import struck him immediately. He bent over the diver and turned off the hydrant.

"You wanted to what?" he asked quietly.

"That fucking bird . . . you know, the second mate . . . just a bloody kiss and maybe a bit of a cuddle . . . Oh, Christ, my fucking head . . ." He shook it and his vision cleared. His eyes focused on the mate's face. A sudden intelligence was stirring him. "That fucking captain! He hit me! The bastard hit me! He can't do that, can't push me around. Christ, he could have killed me, the bastard . . ."

Hobden straightened up. "You get to bed Walker. Go on, fuck off down below." He watched Walker get painfully to his feet and, without offering active assistance. Hobden saw him to his bunk. Then he returned to the officers' accommodation through the internal alleyways. He entered the officer's flat by an accommodation ladder that emerged opposite Susan Paulin's cabin. The door was wide open, swinging slightly as *Active* rolled gently. A faint female scent emanated from the darkened cabin. He knew she was not on the bridge and that Sobey had the anchor watch. He was puzzled and then heard the low tone of voices from the captain's cabin forward. He padded silently along the alleyway and stopped outside. Through the curtain he heard the voices of Susan and Naismith.

He stopped and listened. At first their conversation was low and cautious. Then he heard Naismith raise his slightly. There was a note of unfamiliar passion in it. "Christ, Susan, you realise there's no turning back now! We've burned our boats well and truly!"

And then he heard her reply. It too had passion in it, but what was more significant to Hobden was its tone of equality; "Yes, but what else *could* we do? It's so important to be true to ourselves."

Chapter Thirteen

Naismith woke to a curious feeling of contentment. The enormity of what he had done in the early hours of that day did not strike him with the fear he had expected. Instead a sense of freedom pervaded him, of having risen above pettiness in an access of pride. Suddenly the huge irony of having kept his head down in order to safeguard his pension in a world which was disintegrating seemed extraordinarily funny. The well-trained and cautious side of his nature compelled him to seek for a sinister side to this tremendous elation, but he could not attribute it even to a sense of euphoria.

No, he had made a momentous decision and woken with the conviction that he had done the right thing. So it appeared had Susan. Considering that she had had an unwelcome intruder at her door in the small hours of the night she looked remarkably attractive at breakfast. Her hazel eyes sparkled more than usual and they caught Naismith's more than once during the course of the meal.

But Naismith was not the only one to notice this brightness of manner in the second officer. Hobden remarked it in the captain too, and after the overheard conversation he drew from it the conclusion that Naismith and Susan had become lovers.

Casquets lighthouse, Naismith discovered, could

take five thousand litres of water and would welcome a substantial quantity of diesel oil. In a moderate south-westerly breeze that threatened worse to come, *Active* anchored south of the lighthouse and worked her boats in and out of the eastern gut, pumping first water and then oil ashore. It represented something of a change of plan for Hobden but that was not unusual in the service of BNAS and he was in any case preoccupied by his nocturnal discovery. It seemed, as the day progressed, that there was ample evidence to support his misapprehension. A strange elation possessed Naismith and Susan which was very noticeable to Hobden and fed the jealousy growing in him.

The fact that the Casquets lighthouse had required fuel had not entirely been a fortuitous discovery, but the serious deterioration in the weather that evening was. So too was the fact that it was a Saturday and any irregular movements of the *Active* were unlikely to register at headquarters until Campbell returned to duty on Monday morning. Although the duty officer in the control room would monitor their operations he was sufficiently junior to accept them as being quite in order. Masters of BNAS ships were not exactly notorious for disobedience. Nor, Naismith mused happily, would it appear at all irregular if *Active* anchored off St Peter Port in the lee of Guernsey while the approaching depression passed up-Channel. Already the wind had backed south-westerly and was building up to gale strength. *Active* was lifting her stern and shouldering forward as the seas ran up under her quarter, only to lift her bows skywards as they passed beneath her and she slowed into the troughs. Astern of her, three stormy petrels dangled their tiny webbed feet in the following seas.

In "manufacturing" the work at the Casquets, Naismith had taken the most important decision psychologically. The fact that the lighthouse required a substantial quantity of oil and water simply disguised the fact that he had consciously sought out a job which would detain them in the area. To Captain-Superintendent Campbell it would appear as an excess of zeal but to Naismith's seaman's mind it was one more piece of evidence that fate smiled on his enterprise and had directed him to take upon himself the task of unmasking what he was beginning to think of as a crime against humanity.

He had gone over and over the facts and from the very first, he saw evidence of predestination in the fact that of all the ships navigating their way out of the foggy Channel that night it had been *Wallenstein* that had been so conspicuously sunk. He ignored the fact that perhaps twenty other ships might have successfully made a passage carrying a multitude of other substances or artefacts harmful to some section of the human race. None of those others had subsequently attracted his notice. They were outside the pale of his fate. And as if to confirm this sense of providential intervention a gale was now blowing which would further delay his leaving the area.

He could hardly contain himself until the phone call from Susan's friend due at one the following morning, and with a certain impatience he waved her into his cabin shortly after midnight and shut the door.

There was nothing in Naismith's behaviour to persuade the watching Hobden that he was engaged in anything other than an affair with his second officer.

"Hullo, darling . . . yes. Did you find out anything?" There was a long pause during which Susan scribbled on a piece of paper. Naismith was surprised she knew shorthand and then wondered why he should be. He poured out two drinks. A small cognac for her and a large whisky for himself. It was unusual for him to drink at sea but then, as he had observed twenty-four hours earlier, he had burnt his boats and the Rubicon lay behind him.

Susan put the phone down and expelled a long breath.

"Well?"

"It's worse than we think. *Wallenstein* isn't the first ship with a consignment of that stuff. She's the third. Thanks." She took the cognac and sipped it.

"Peter found out a number of things. First he pursued the St Peter Port side. Both men are dead; the symptoms were recorded as those of poisoning from some form of shellfish but there is to be no autopsy . . ." Naismith looked out of the cabin window. The lights of St Peter Port were a mile away. So were two corpses and a crewless fishing boat called the *Three Brothers*. For a second he imagined he might land and learn more, but the wildness of the night and the futility of such a course of action made him dismiss the idea.

"Then," Susan continued, "he got onto the makers of the television report about the news of the nerve gas. It was a West German film team led by a man called Harald Dietz. The report he syndicated was only a part of some investigations he's been carrying out about the use of such chemicals in warfare. He's found that they are stockpiled in West Germany and he's not too happy about this. Apparently there's a firm that makes industrial and agricultural chemicals that is suspected of manufacturing this sort of thing."

"Bloody hell!"

"Yes, it's not a very pleasant story is it? Odd that the stuff is going out on Liberian ships, though . . ."

"Not really. They might be owned by almost anyone."

"True. 'The unacceptable face of capitalism'."

"Anything else?"

"Not really. He says he's had no luck about discovering whether *Harwich* got all the drums back, but his usual contact at the Ministry of Defence went very odd when Peter did a bit of probing."

"Odd?"

"Yes. Peter says," she looked at the scribbled shorthand, "'I took him to lunch, deciding that a face-to-face confrontation would be best and his reaction was odd. Odd enough to convince me that something was wrong.'"

"Your Peter sounds a very thorough man."

"I told you he was."

"Right. Well that just about squares everything up doesn't it?" He paused then looked her in the eye. "Susan. *If* we get that drum up, and it's a pretty big *if*, we may be in a lot of trouble. Particularly as, whatever or whoever is behind this thing, the British Government must be involved. Why else was *Harwich* at the wreck? I daresay we're doing it at the behest of the Americans but we could be in pretty awful hot water. Lose our jobs."

"I don't care, sir, not for myself. I realise it is much worse for you but I feel so strongly about it that the job isn't that important."

He smiled at her. "No, you told me that last night, too."

"If you want to drop the whole thing I'd quite

understand. I mean we've given the idea to Peter and it's certain to get publicity now."

"That doesn't alter the fact that there's a drum of that stuff lying on the seabed and we know that it's terribly lethal even in heavily diluted doses. It could conceivably be disturbed by a trawl . . ."

"D'you think we can retrieve it?"

Naismith sniffed. "I don't know. But I do know we can try."

The gale lasted twelve hours. By the Sunday morning the wind had swung into the north west and died to a chilly breeze which made the Channel sparkle under puffs of cumulus. By the afternoon *Active* was approaching the site of the wreck of the *Wallenstein*.

Naismith stood on the bridge and looked down on the boat deck. Scranton had swallowed the lie and was even now preparing his gear in the motor boat as it lay at the rail waiting to be lowered.

"We've had a message requesting us to make an attempt to find a missing drum of that chemical, Mr Scranton. Now, we're not supposed to know that what's in it is lethal," he had said earlier in the privacy of his cabin, "so if you don't want to go down I'll understand and can probably cover for you . . ."

"That's all right Captain. I'm sure that the time lapse has washed it all away and I'm not bothered. I'll be glad of something to do."

"You can send that young bastard Walker down if you like."

"Him?" Scranton smiled contemptuously. "He can tend my lines. He's not fit for much more. He was kicked off North Sea work, you know . . ."

Naismith smile to himself. He had appealed to

176

Scranton's vanity and triumphed. The diver was eager to re-establish his reputation, particularly where he thought he had lost it. Naismith watched the boat pull away from the ship and went into the wheelhouse. *Active*, under easy revs, held expertly between wind and tide, contrived to maintain her position three quarters of a mile away from the position of the wreck of the *Wallenstein*. From the seabed came back the lonely ping of the sonar response from her broken hull. Susan hopped attentively about from the Decca to the sonar and back to the chart table. Hobden was absent. There was no need for his presence on the bridge but it was unusual. Still, Naismith reflected, the mate was a busy man and Chas' aversion to small talk was still known. Besides, it was best that only the conspirators were present when the "crime" was being perpetrated.

Susan raised her head from the radar visor. "Boat's on the spot, sir."

Naismith raised the handset. "Motor boat – *Active*, you are on the spot."

"Roger." He saw Sobey wave his hand and the boat's crew lowered their one-hundred-weight sinker to the seabed as a shot line for Scranton. The tide was slack and Scranton lost no time in diving. Naismith settled down to wait. Twenty minutes later they saw Scranton surface, watched him hauled into the boat and have his air tanks changed. Naismith resisted the temptation to request a situation report from Sobey. He looked at his watch. Slack water was over. He had to increase engine revolutions to maintain station. The driver disappeared.

"Scranton's pushing his luck," he muttered to himself. Suddenly he saw Scranton's head bobbing alongside the boat again. Eager hands hauled him inboard and there was some sorting out of gear. The handset crackled to life.

"Motor boat to *Active*. Bull's-eye."

Naismith's hand was shaking as he lifted the VHF radio. "Well done," he said, matter-of-factly. "Haul in your shot line and I'll come alongside and take it off you."

"Roger." He turned to find Susan beside him.

"I don't believe it," she said.

"Neither do I," he said, "but it's true. Call the bosun to stand-by on the foredeck and we'll lift it on board." Their eyes met. If they damaged the drum they were all as good as dead.

"Aye, aye, sir."

"Motor boat to *Active* – we're aweigh and all ready for you."

"Roger." He pushed the engine controllers to half speed. "Port easy . . . midships. steady as she goes." He stopped the engines as *Active* edged up to the waiting boat. A heaving line snaked out from the tender's side and was caught by the boat's crew. Naismith put the engines astern. The hull trembled as the ship lost way. The bosun's gang hauled in the heaving line and then the heavier polypropylene. Hobden arrived on the foredeck. The rope was transferred from boat to deck.

"Let's have the service derrick outboard ready, Bosun," Hobden took charge and the light after derrick on the port side was swung expectantly outboard. The polypropylene rope had come tight and Able Seaman Ellice took a turn and hove it up by the after drum. Naismith leaned over the bridge wing with Susan beside him. Both held their breath.

Suddenly the drum broke surface. An innocuous

178

green drum with "Dry-Cleaning Fluid" stencilled conspicuously on it in white and the port of destination, *Santa Maria*. There was a company logo reminiscent of the Legs of Man. "Avast now!" bawled Hobden to Ellice and then to the boat's crew.

"Come on then, hook the purchase in . . ."

Sobey's boat came alongside and the derrick purchase was hooked in to prevent damaging the drum as it came over the ship's side. Two minutes later it stood on the deck.

"Let's have the bloody thing lashed, then," Hobden said savagely.

"Wonder who's been chewing *his* balls?" muttered Ellice as he passed a lashing.

"Miss Susie Paulin perhaps," answered Harris, grinning obscenely.

"You're a daft bastard Harris. That would make even Hobden smile . . ."

"Cut that dirty talk you two," snapped Mr Jones, the bosun.

On the bridge Naismith steadied *Active* on a course up-Channel, heaving a sigh of relief. He still could not quite believe his luck. His calculations must have been absolutely . . .

"Sir." He looked out onto the port bridge wing. Susan Paulin was facing aft and her face expressed serious concern.

"Put her on autopilot, Quartermaster," he said to Potts and moved out to join her. She pointed astern.

"I think we've been spotted."

The plane completed its turn and was coming towards them at low altitude. They watched it grow larger, ignoring the laughter coming up from the boat deck where the boat's crew and diver were clearing the gear out of the boat and congratulating themselves.

The Nimrod roared overhead at mast height.

"D'you think they're taking photographs?" Susan asked suddenly.

Naismith looked over the bridge front. The drum stood lashed against the hatch coaming, its white stencilled legend and logo turned conveniently outboard. A worm of foreboding twisted uneasily in his stomach and he looked at Susan.

"Whatever happens, Susan, remember this; that we only think that stuff is a toxic chemical. We don't *know* it is nerve gas. At least until we get ashore and make contact with your friend."

"Why d'you say that, sir?"

"Because I think our luck just ran out."

Chapter Fourteen

"You were bleeding wrong, weren't you Pottsy, eh?" taunted Harris as the deck hands sat in the mess decks enjoying their Smoke-Oh.

Quartermaster Potts, who had just come down from the bridge at four o'clock, ignored the remark. He sipped his pint of tea and rolled himself a cigarette.

"H-bomb, my arse," Harris continued, leering round at the other seamen who sat around the table.

"Why don't you shut up, Harris!" said one, quietly. "It's quite obvious that a lot of trouble went into getting that bloody drum up. I reckon Pottsy's got it more or less right. It's the navy that want that drum up . . ."

"That's why Pottsy's sub was interested . . ."

"Yeah, and that bleeding destroyer . . ."

"Funny they didn't get it, though, ain't it? I mean all that electronic crap aboard those ships and it's the old *Active* that comes along and hits it spot on."

"Clever bastard the Old Man."

"The Old Man's a prick," said Harris.

"Yeah," agreed another, "but he's a clever prick, Harris, not an ordinary one like you."

"Well done, Mr Scranton." Naismith shook the smiling diver's hand.

"Thank you, Captain." Scranton looked pleased.

181

"You dropped me right on it. I went out from the shot line on a fifty foot radius, nothing. Increased to eighty and bingo! As Bob Sobey said, a bull's-eye."

"A bloody good show, anyway."

"I suppose the matter's classified, eh? I mean there's a fair bit of speculation among the lads."

Naismith nodded. "Best kept quiet, I think. Now," he went on changing the subject, "I propose landing you at St Peter Port and you can fly back to the mainland."

"There's no hurry, Captain . . ."

"I want Walker off the ship." He turned to see the mate. "Hullo Chas, I was telling Mr Scranton here that we'll land him at Peter Port."

"I heard." Hobden turned abruptly away leaving Naismith nonplussed.

"He's decided against making a complaint against you, Captain," put in Scranton.

"Eh? Oh, well he wouldn't have got very far with it, considering what he was up to . . ." Naismith did not add that he would feel happier when Scranton was ashore too.

Frank Davis lay on his bunk and stared at the photograph of Juanita. He wondered where she was now and suppressed the rising panic in his stomach with the thought that he had only a week more to do aboard the *Active*. Then he would be free, free to cross the Atlantic, abandon his futile project of raising a family in a country for whom he felt nothing but indifference.

"Hey Frank!" His cabin door burst open and the excited face of Ordinary Seaman Ellice stared at him. "They're on about Costa Maya on the telly!" Davis swung his legs over the bunk and followed Ellice into the mess deck.

The television showed a cloud of dust which cleared slowly. ". . . Government sources said here today that they had driven back the rebel offensive and that it represented a final thrust by the insurgents before the inevitable end of the uprising . . ." A close-up of steel-helmeted artillerymen showed up as they loaded a shell into the breech of a field-gun. Behind them a tank moved forward. The news reporter's voice went on, "But unofficial sources usually held to be reliable, stated that considerable numbers of left-wing militia are still advancing upon Santa Maria and the claim a week ago that the junta were in control of the countryside was inaccurate propaganda. All that is known for certain is that American-supplied F4 fighter bombers have been flying a series of almost continuous sorties to the westward from Santa Maria . . ." A fighter streaked across the screen. ". . . At least two of these aircraft are known to have been shot down and militia sources claim six. These sources also claim an extensive use of nerve gas against concentrations of population. With the refugee problem acute on the borders, the situation in Costa Maya is rapidly felt to be approaching crisis point. The main concern here is what the reaction from the United States will be now that the Presidential Election campaign is also reaching its crisis . . ."

"Not too good, eh Frank?" Ellice said, smiling kindly at the taciturn Liverpudlian for whom he had conceived a degree of respect.

"No, not too good at all."

They were abeam of the Cherbourg peninsula by dawn, having landed Scranton, Walker and their gear at St Peter Port the night before. Naismith would undoubtedly incur Campbell's displeasure at the unnecessary extravagance of the airfares, but he could justify them on the grounds of Walker's conduct. BNAS would have to pay for the privilege of employing women, he thought with a wry smile.

Naismith heard the aircraft as he shaved. He ran to his cabin window in time to see the second Nimrod climb and bank away from them. Buzzing by Nimrods was not exactly unusual but Naismith knew this was no casual interception to check if they were an illegal fishing boat. The Ministry of Defence wanted to know the whereabouts of *Active*. Well they knew, and the next move was up to them. It came sooner than he expected. Before he had wiped the lather off his face the Satcomm phone rang. He strode into the dayroom and picked it up.

"*Active*, Captain . . ."

"Is that . . . is that . . . the Captain?" The voice sounded muffled.

"Yes." He strained to hear what was normally a crystal-clear link.

"This is Peter, Captain, no more names, okay? Tell the third party the matter's come to a head. The heavies hit me last night. Too many questions was the explanation . . ."

"Are you all right?" Naismith's heart had begun to pound.

"No, I'm not. You've stuck a needle in a raw nerve, Captain. The shit's hit the fan. I've had my lot, the rest is coming your way."

"Are you going to follow the matter further?"

"No. Can't be done . . . got to go now. Tell you-know-who I'm all right and Captain . . ."

"Yes?"

"Get her back in one piece."

The line went dead. Naismith stood holding the handset, stupidly staring at it. "Oh, my God . . ." he muttered.

Harwich found them at noon. She came tearing down from the north with a great bone in her teeth. Naismith had been watching for her and was already on the bridge. He had idled the morning away, making sure the VHF radios were turned down and casting frequent glances in the direction of the English coast, over the horizon to the north.

In company with half a dozen other ships *Active* was approaching the narrow traffic lane that north-east bound shipping was obliged to take through the Dover Strait, running up the French coast from the Greenwich meridian to the Sandettié Banks off Calais.

Naismith watched the destroyer close them. *Harwich* was capable of almost twice the speed of *Active*. He felt stupidly helpless. A feeling of vacillation and foolishness filled him.

What had he done? What were the consequences going to be for Wendy and the children? What on earth was he trying to prove?

But he knew that. He was trying to stop people being destroyed by barbaric means, for wanting the most basic of human rights. The fact that he was defying the authorities of his own country only showed the enormity of the problem and the strange ramifications of power politics. If Peter was right and the British Government were engaged in some cynical trade-off with their American allies the matter should not be secret. That was not democracy. All the evidence argued the accuracy of Susan's friend's information. The dilemma occasioned by opposing loyalties seemed to lessen its grip on him. He did not have to make a choice between the lesser of two evils. The only thing to do was to oppose what was wrong.

"That destroyer, sir," said Sobey with a puzzled look on his face," she seems to be closing us."

Naismith nodded. "Yes. I'll keep an eye on her. You'll be wanting to hand over to Susan now."

"Yes, sir."

"Go ahead." He raised his glasses and watched *Harwich* closing them. Behind him in the wheelhouse the watch changed. An aldis began winking at them from *Harwich*'s starboard bridge wing. He ignored it, reflecting that *Active*'s hands would be in the mess deck getting their dinner. There would not be too many witnesses to this encounter. Susan came and stood beside him.

"This is what we've been waiting for, sir."

"Yes."

"What do you think he's going to do?"

"I don't know but I think you had better turn the volume up on the VHF radios."

It was clear that the naval rating had been calling them for some time, his voice was weary and unenthusiastic.

"*Active*, *Active*, *Active*, this is warship *Harwich*, come in please, over."

Naismith delayed a moment longer. The long lean hull of the destroyer swung onto a parallel course to *Active*, her bow level with *Active*'s bridge. The washes of both ships slapped together as *Harwich* reduced her speed to that of her quarry. Naismith picked up the handset.

"Warship *Harwich*, this is *Active*. What are your intentions?"

"*Active*, this is warship *Harwich*, stand-by . . ." The operator, surprised at last to get a response, had now to consult an officer. Naismith crossed to the autopilot and altered the course setting. *Active* began a slow swing to port, across *Harwich*'s bow. Raising his glasses Naismith could clearly see the officer of the watch notice what had happened. He saw, equally clearly, Captain Troughton's attention drawn to it. *Harwich*'s sharply raked bow swung in towards *Active*'s quarter. Naismith reset the autopilot to the original course and *Active* sat immediately ahead of her pursuer. Quartermaster Potts was looking oddly at Naismith.

"Just seeing if my taxes are being properly expended, Mr Potts, testing the navy's reflexes." Potts' frown deepened. He looked at Susan.

"Don't worry, Mr Potts," she said very matter-of-factly, "Captain Naismith is just doing his duty."

Potts shrugged, picked up the tin of Brasso and began to burnish *Active*'s wheelhouse brass.

Harwich swung out on *Active*'s quarter again and increased speed, coming up into her former position. The VHF came to life.

"*Active, Active*, this is warship *Harwich*. You will please stop your vessel. I repeat you will stop your vessel. Over."

"Get on that radio, Susan. I want it cool and very feminine. Ask . . . no tell him, to repeat." Susan nodded. She was very pale.

"Please repeat your message, *Harwich*. Over." There was a pause.

"Good afternoon, *Active*. You must stop your ship at once . . ." The voice was clearly Dartmouth elocuted. Naismith nodded with satisfaction.

"Tell him you must first inform the master."

"*Harwich*, *Harwich*, this is *Active*. You wish me to stop my ship, is that correct?" Susan winked at Naismith.

A sigh came over the destroyer's carrier and then a voice said in a tone of strained patience, "That is correct, *Active*. Stop your ship."

Susan giggled. "Oh, are you serious? I thought you wanted to carry out an exercise on me . . ." she smothered her mouth to suppress a fit of real laughter.

"That, my girl, was a real *double entendre*." Naismith said grinning despite himself. But the navy were not amused.

"This is an operational order. You should stop at once, *Active*."

"*Harwich*, this is *Active*. Wait one while I inform the master." She lowered the handset. "Phew."

"Well done."

"D'you think it was a good idea to make them mad?"

"No, but that lot went out on Channel 16 for the whole world to hear." He took the radio from her. "I shall now be brisk and outraged." He spoke into the mouthpiece. "*Harwich*, *Harwich*, this is *Active*, please go to Channel 6."

They both shifted channels then Naismith said, "This is the master speaking. I understand you wish me to stop my ship. Is this to return the photographs? Over."

"No, Captain it is not!" The voice sounded like *Harwich*'s first lieutenant. He was clearly as angry as on their last meeting. "We require you to stop your ship and receive a boarding party. Over."

"I'm sorry, *Harwich*, but I cannot comply and question your authority to board me."

"I assure you, Captain, we have ample authority to board you. Now please stop your vessel."

"May I please speak to Captain Troughton? Over."

There was a silence and then Troughton's urbane voice came over the air. Naismith could see him through the glasses with the handset to his mouth.

"Afternoon, Captain. Please comply with my request; failure to do so could result in the most serious consequences."

"I would like to know why you wish to board, Captain Troughton. Over."

"Please stop playing games, Naismith, and stop your engines."

"This ship has done nothing illegal, Captain, and I am questioning your right to board me on the high seas."

No reply came from *Harwich* but Naismith saw her increase speed and ease again as their bridges came abreast. To a casual observer it did indeed look as though an exercise was in progress. *Harwich* towered over *Active*, her thick masts and bedstead radars turning remorselessly above them. Naismith went out on the port bridge wing. "Take the wheel, Mr Potts, course oh-eight-oh and nothing to port!"

"Oh-eight-oh and nothing to port, sir." Potts took the wheel with a sense of relief. At such a time it was best to be doing something.

Naismith picked up the megaphone and stood waiting for Troughton. He suddenly appeared on *Harwich*'s starboard bridge wing.

"What the hell d'you think you're playing at, Naismith? You know damned well I can stop you *and* board you."

"That's as maybe, Captain, but I've an equal right to know why."

"I'm not in the debating business, I'm ordering you to stop." Naismith noticed two other men behind Troughton. One, who seemed to be in khaki had a pair of glasses to his eyes while the other, who wore no discernible uniform, pointed onto *Active*'s foredeck.

"I know you want the drum off us, Troughton, but it's legitimately acquired salvage and you can't touch it."

There was no reply from Troughton but he had withdrawn slightly and appeared to be consulting with someone. Naismith hoped Troughton would ascribe to him commercial motives.

"Is it legitimately acquired salvage, sir?" asked Susan doubtfully.

"I don't know, but I'm willing to bet neither does Troughton." He saw Troughton raise his own megaphone.

"Captain," he said reasonably, "the drum is a Droit of the Crown . . ."

"Rubbish!" shouted Naismith. "How can a drum of cleaning fluid from a German ship be a Droit of the Crown when recovered in international waters? And if it is very *valuable* cleaning fluid, Captain Troughton, then the salvors are entitled to their fair share of its value."

There was another pause during which Hobden appeared on the bridge.

"What the hell's going on?" Susan heard him and turned.

"It's all right, Chas, the Captain's having an argument with the captain of that destroyer. He won't give up that drum of cleaning fluid on the foredeck."

Hobden looked down at her. Since he had learned of her affair with Naismith she had revolted him.

190

"And you think that's all right?" He pushed past her and approached Naismith just as Troughton raised his megaphone again.

"Captain, you don't understand. It is absolutely essential that you stop your ship. You and your crew are endangered by the chemical in that drum. It is a very potent industrial chemical and we have to repossess it at once."

Troughton's announcement had had an effect elsewhere on *Active*. Attracted by the unusual events, most of *Active*'s crew had abandoned the mess and were lining the port rail. A sullen murmur began to be heard from them on her bridge.

Naismith thought quickly. His own innate sense of caution began to assert itself. Things had, perhaps gone far enough. Now *Harwich* was alongside he could prevaricate but not prevent. Ashore Peter had already paid part of the price of challenging government, they might yet make a big enough stink about the pollution issue once they had mobilised the environmental lobby. It was time, he thought, to cash in his insurance policy.

"Captain Troughton," he called through his megaphone, "I am a seaman engaged in the preservation of safety at sea. The carriage of that drum represents an unacceptable risk to the safety of seamen and the purity of the oceans. I mean to take it ashore and expose the carriage of such substances. The drum is perfectly safe aboard my ship." He lowered the megaphone, knowing that he had blown the idea of being a greedy salvor. Now Troughton would assume he was a crank.

He could see Troughton was taken aback just as he was aware of Susan's enthusiastic support beside him. But Troughton had clearly decided he was dealing with a blockhead of an idealist. He was also doubly aware that the drum *had* to be recovered.

"Captain Naismith, you are an officer in Government Service. You are obliged to obey my instructions. *You must stop your ship!*"

"I am a private individual, Captain Troughton, and you may go to hell!" He lowered the megaphone and turned away just as Hobden came out onto the bridge wing.

"What the hell is going on?" asked the big man.

Chapter Fifteen

Frank Davis was one of the first seamen on deck after the cook had shouted below that "A bloody great destroyer was alongside." Nobody thought anything was wrong until Troughton and Naismith began abusing each other through their megaphones. Then speculation ran wild; the hydrogen bomb theory was aired again until Davis guessed the obvious. His theory about the drum of "cleaning fluid" was almost immediately confirmed by the two captains and while the other hands were confused, Davis was seized by a sudden desire to participate in this showdown with the powerful. Detaching himself from his arguing shipmates he made his way towards the bridge.

Naismith turned on Hobden and ordered him to pipe down, but Hobden's confusion was fuelled by his sudden violent dislike of Naismith. Naismith was the man who succeeded both professionally and sexually, that cheated able men like himself of advancement and love. On top of this twin disappointment there now came the clear perception that something very irregular was going on aboard *Active*. Unlike the passive and detached Potts, to whom the current events were of only objective interest, Hobden was anxious to get to the root of the matter. As the chief mate his sense of the possessive over the ship was even stronger than Naismith's, and his obsession with Susan and his growing jealousy of the captain now came boiling to a head.

"What the hell is going on?" he repeated, his big shoulders hunching aggressively.

"For Christ's sake shut up, Chas, I'm trying to think . . ."

Susan came forward. "It's all right Chas, really, the Captain is only trying to stop something awful happening . . ."

Hobden turned on the girl disbelievingly. Above the huge bristling beard his eyebrows drew together in a terrible frown.

"Are you both bloody mad? If he," he nodded towards the *Harwich* which seemed to be pulling slightly away from *Active* and dropping slowly astern, "if he wants the ship stopped then you should stop her!"

He moved towards the controllers but Susan blocked him. "No!" He pushed her aside and she fell. Naismith turned at her cry.

"God damn you, Hobden, *I* command here!"

"Not if you're insane, mister." Hobden's hand reached out for the controllers again and Naismith lunged at him. Hobden grabbed the captain forcing him backwards; holding Naismith off with one powerful arm he felled him with a right to the chin. Naismith went over backwards and struck his head on the steel bulwark.

Hobden stared down at his handiwork for a moment and then his attention was taken by the roar that filled the air. *Harwich* had swung round and lifting off her quarter deck was the black shape of a Lynx helicopter.

*   *   *

Davis arrived on the bridge via the starboard ladder. He wanted to know what was going on without receiving an abrupt rebuff that an approach up the port ladder would have drawn from a preoccupied Captain Naismith. The starboard side was deserted and he cautiously entered the wheelhouse, almost tripping over Susan Paulin as she got to her feet. She saw who it was and Davis helped her up.

"What's going on like, sec?" Susan decided it was time to end the captain's caution. She levelled with the seaman:

"Your wife, Davis, someone's shipping bloody nerve gas out to drop on people like your wife. We've got a drum of it on the foredeck and that naval ship wants it back . . . wants to hush it up . . ."

Davis' mouth dropped open as Susan noticed Naismith's head had hit the bulwark and the captain lay inert. "Bloody hell!" She propelled Davis forward, through the opposite door of the wheelhouse and out onto the bridge wing. Hobden was just turning away from the approaching helicopter, moving into the wheelhouse to stop the ship and call the *Harwich* on VHF, when Susan shouted, "You've got to stop the mate, Davis! Stop the mate!"

Impelled by pent-up worry, hatred and outrage, Davis moved forward fast. His right shoulder struck the astonished Hobden in the chest and he staggered backwards. The head-butt caught him as he tried to recover and reeling uncertainly he lost his footing at the top of the port ladder. Like a pole-axed bull, Hobden crashed unconscious to the deck below. Davis disappeared after him and Susan came out onto the bridge wing, herself suddenly conscious of the roar of the Lynx as it came to the hover over *Active*'s helicopter flight deck.

She watched terrified as a rope emerged and hung down onto *Active*'s deck. Then a man, two men, three, began absailing expertly down it. They wore khaki and the green berets of marines, and they carried automatic weapons.

Naismith came to in the knowledge that *Active* was stopped. His eyes fluttered open, closed, then opened again. His brow contracted with the pain in his head.

He tried to get slowly to his feet, to think, but a shadow fell over him and the black muzzle of a machine gun jolted his teeth.

"Get up slowly with your hands on your head." The voice was precise, devoid of sentiment. He did as he was bid, his head swimming and the gorge rising in his throat. His eyes cleared and he was aware of his bridge swarming with armed men. He tried to count them and eventually resolved the number to six. They stood in the wheelhouse, their automatic weapons covering Potts and Susan.

He looked round. *Active* and *Harwich* both lay stopped, the big destroyer almost alongside. Naismith felt himself pushed forward and turned on the marine angrily. "Stop that!"

"Shut your mouth, Captain." The voice was curt and clearly that of an officer. "You've caused us a great deal of trouble." He turned aside. "Corporal, take Lay and Crowhurst and get that drum ready to go."

"Sir!" Three men broke away.

"Let these two go, lieutenant," said Naismith through swelling lips, nodding at Susan and Potts. "They have only obeyed orders." The marine officer ignored him. There was a call on a portable radio and one of the marines bent his head to answer it.

"Roger!"

The man advanced and whispered in the officer's ear. Both men moved swiftly to the bridge front. By twisting round where he was, Naismith could see the drum on the foredeck. Davis was poised over it with a heavy marline spike and a hammer. He was shouting something across the hundred feet of water that separated the two ships. Naismith suddenly heard Troughton's voice through a megaphone:

"Take him out!"

The marine officer ordered one of his men to take aim.

"If you make a balls of that," Naismith said, "that man has grievance enough to kill us all." He saw the marine hesitate and went on. "Let me send the Quartermaster here to clear all my men off the upper deck, then I'll go down and talk to him and you can have your bloody drum."

The marine officer considered for a moment then turned to his radio operator and said, "Tell the Captain that I'll handle it . . ."

"Sir?" Naismith looked at Susan. She looked dishevelled, he noticed, as though she too had been knocked down. "Sir, I think if you let me go down and talk to Davis he'll listen to me . . ."

Naismith addressed the marine officer. "Miss Paulin's right lieutenant, let her go and talk to the man. He'll resent me and most certainly won't capitulate to force . . ."

The officer nodded. "Okay, Captain, but any funny nonsense and you won't live to regret it."

"Neither will you, lieutenant, if that man down there punctures that drum . . ." His own equanimity amazed him and he smiled at Susan as she and Potts left the bridge with a marine for company.

Naismith was alone with the officer and his radio operator. The ringing in his head had given way to an insistent buzzing and he became aware of the Lynx sitting out on their other quarter, covering the boarding party with yet another machine gun. It struck him as immensely funny, all this destructive fire power against the impotent *Active* and himself. Himself and a strong-willed girl, of course, and he looked forward to see Susan emerge onto the foredeck.

All thought of laughter vanished as swiftly as it had come. He saw Davis shake his head and heard him shout something. Susan advanced a little and Davis's hand lifted the hammer above the spike. Susan stopped and there were some words between them.

Then there was a sharp crack and Davis' head was blown apart.

Chapter Sixteen

"Good morning, Captain." The naval steward was cheerfully attentive as he placed the breakfast tray on the small table-locker. "There's shaving tackle, sir and," he pulled aside the incongruous floral curtain and revealed a porthole, "a fine view of Pompey."

"Where's my ship?"

"Anchored at Spithead, sir."

"Is there anyone else on board here from her?"

"Don't know sir. If you require anything else please ring." He indicated the bell and left Naismith.

He toyed with a half-slice of toast and drank two cups of coffee and tried to recall what had happened the previous afternoon. He was very confused about certain items and knew he had been drugged after he had come aboard *Harwich*. Perhaps it was to make him sleep but he wondered if he might not have been given a truth-drug like Pentathol. There had been a rather hatchet-faced civilian with Captain Troughton when the marine officer had eventually brought him aboard.

Naismith tried to reconstruct what had occurred after Davis's death. He remembered screaming abuse at the marine and then Hobden appeared, one eye contused and an expression of complete bewilderment on his face. Then he remembered an uncontrollable Susan sobbing in his arms as she alternated between remorse and vitriolic condemnation of the representatives of authority.

In company with Harwich they had got the ship under way, their marine guests remaining as "prize crew" and with *Harwich* as escort they had proceeded towards Portsmouth. The marine officer had been his constant companion, saying hardly a word, although there appeared to be no interference with the rest of the crew. Before he had been taken off the night before, he had officially handed over the ship to Hobden. It had been an icily formal affair and Naismith had merely endorsed the instructions passed to them from *Harwich*.

There was to be no communication ashore, no messages to BNAS, nothing. *Active* was to remain at anchor. Had Naismith been less preoccupied with his own immediate future he might have noticed the contrition in Hobden's expression. Still choking over his misapprehensions about the captain's conduct, he had learned from Susan during her suitably adapted explanation of events to the officers in the wardroom, what had been going on during her nocturnal visits to Naismith. Susan had stuck to Naismith's instruction that their recovery of the drum might be represented as quixotic, but she must not give grounds for it appearing that either had suspected it contained anything worse than a toxic and polluting industrial chemical.

She had no compunction in adopting this story now that Naismith was under what amounted to arrest, and that Davis was dead. She talked fast and eloquently to protect Naismith and to blot out the horror of what had happened in front of her eyes. And although Hobden might damn her for her lunacy in pushing her insane anti-pollution ideas so far, reminding her that she worked for BNAS not a crackpot ecological outfit, he began to feel remorse for his own action in striking Naismith, and sympathy for Susan before whom Davis had been so horribly murdered.

Naismith wondered how they had explained their actions over himself. He remembered that the Lynx that airlifted him across to *Harwich* had deposited a civilian gentleman aboard *Active* "to give the men a pep talk, old man," Troughton had explained in his genteel murderer's voice as Naismith stood in his cabin. He had sensed the embarrassment of Troughton, that the navy had gone too far, assuming that Naismith had known he was playing fast and loose with nerve gas agent. Yet they had no evidence to accuse him of doing so. Besides, that would have revealed everything.

He did not receive much of an interrogation that evening. Just a few general questions, then they had given him cocoa with something in it and whisked him off to this tiny cabin.

He shaved and dressed. Black uniform trousers and shoes, a stained shirt and black tie and the pullover with the four gold bars of master on his shoulders.

They had not let him bring his cap and he felt curiously naked without it. The detail worried him and he realised it worried him because he did not want to think of the thing that concerned his most of all: the death of Davis.

There was a strong sense of anticlimax upon him, anticlimax as to the turn events had taken and mixed with culpability; for he did not believe his career would survive what had taken place yesterday. But above all there was guilt. It was not just guilt for the death of Davis, although that lay over all like a pall, but guilt for abandoning the caution he had made almost a tenet of faith, guilt for becoming *involved* in the whole wretched matter, and guilt for being influenced by Susan. "It won't make the slightest difference," he had said to the objecting Hobden when he had first heard that they were to have BNAS's first female officer appointed to *Active*. Well he had been proved wrong and Hobden right. And there was the feeling of guilt that it had been his own vanity that had caused his present imbroglio. He saw it all now. The providential discovery, bit by bit, of what was on board the *Wallenstein* had gone hand in hand with the dissolution of his professional integrity. Had he not given way to the stupid, superstitious conviction that he had been irradiated by the light of truth, like some Old Testament prophet, he would not have been so insane as to think he could achieve anything. Fate, if he believed in it at all at that moment, had twisted and accomplished his downfall.

And yet, and yet, what had he and Susan done? They both loved the sea, she with the clear passion of youth, he with a sad realisation that it was too late to prevent the sea being as despoiled as the land. And again he felt anger. Why did men like Troughton not see it? Or did they, and had they abandoned their consciences? What *was* the attraction of violence?

His own son would have far rather spent a day aboard *Harwich* than a day on *Active*. The seminal lust to go a-hunting lay strong within them, he and Ben, Troughton and his superiors, the old men in London, Washington and Moscow. That is why there is no hope, he thought. The monstrous joke fate had played on him it would play on mankind. Everywhere about him he saw signs of it and it seemed that the supine indifference of mankind would allow it to occur. If there was no nuclear exchange then the intolerance and polarisation of political ideologies would provoke more deadly wars like that raging in Costa Maya. And while they occurred, Europe, the Europe that had set the world alight with its energy and philosophies, would waste away under its own acid rain, would strangle itself with its own rubbish and sell death to the ignorant who crowded the market place to buy it.

He thought for a moment he might be going mad and moved to the porthole as though for air. But this was a destroyer, designed to pass through nuclear fallout, and the port would not open. He stared through it. Bobbing alongside a half-dozen black-headed gulls pecked among the galley refuse from *Harwich*. He could see the black smudges of oil upon two of them and even the water alongside the humming hull of the warship showed a faint slick of diesel. No, he was quite sane, and quite convinced he had been right.

The cabin door slid open and Lieutenant Elliott entered. "They're ready for you now, sir."

"What happened to the seaman from *Active* you shot, Lieutenant?"

"I'm not permitted to talk . . ."

"Just tell me where the bullet came from, will you? None of the marines on board *Active* appeared to open fire."

"He was taken out by a shot from a marksman on *Harwich*'s bridge, sir."

"*Taken out*? Christ, Lieutenant, d'you have to learn euphemisms to make your job palatable?"

"Come this way please, sir." Naismith had the satisfaction of seeing the blood flush the nape of Elliott's neck as he followed the lieutenant.

There were three men in Troughton's cabin, the

Captain himself, the hatchet-faced civilian and a small, ascetic man with a high colour and the meticulously tied and minuscule tie knot that declared him a sailor in civilian clothing. Naismith rated him a Rear-Admiral. Their expressions were dead-pan and the hatchet-faced civilian was clearly in charge.

"Do sit down, Captain Naismith." He indicated an upright chair in the centre of the cabin. The other three occupants reclined on a settee and an armchair.

"Now, Captain, this isn't an interrogation, or anything like that, but we must have some answers to explain your highly irregular conduct yesterday afternoon."

"Do my superiors know you removed me from my ship, sir?" he asked.

An icy light flared in the eyes of Hatchet-face. "Captain Naismith I don't think you understand quite what you have done in defying Captain Troughton's order to stop yesterday . . ."

"Are you questioning my refusal to stop, or my refusal to hand over a drum of highly polluting chemical that my divers were successful in raising from a wreck? Are you aware that the Service which employs me is responsible for the safety of navigation, and that includes the protection of seamen on the high seas to pursue their business – no, you damn well hear me out! Those fishermen that died in St Peter Port were poisoned by the filthy stuff on board that damned ship. I have every right, officially, morally and personally, to recover that drum. I abhor the pollution of the seas . . ."

"So do we, Captain," snapped the Rear-Admiral, "hence our efforts to recover it. D'you think we went to the trouble of despatching a Type 42 with

204

a full diving team on board for our own amusement?"

"Indeed not, sir, I found Captain Troughton's attitude led me to suspect there might be something even more suspicious about the *Wallenstein*'s cargo. Indeed the lengths to which you went were extraordinary, culminating as they did in the murder of one of my crew . . ."

He was carried on the wave of his own eloquence, astonished at the renewal of an anger he had thought burnt out in self-pity. He saw the exchange of glances, the colour mount to Troughton's cheeks at the accusation of mismanagement and wondered if he had gone too far. Then Hatchet-face spoke again.

"If you knew the substance in the drum," he said with the pedantry of a civil servant, "was highly toxic, why did you not surrender it?"

"Because I intended to expose the dangers of carrying such cargos and," he added as a masterstroke of ambivalence, "question the necessity of their manufacture."

"A quixotic action for a civil employee of government, wouldn't you say?"

"Even civil servants may pursue their private beliefs. According to the newspapers some do little else."

A fleeting smile crossed the Rear-Admiral's face. "How did you know it was so toxic?" he asked.

"A combination of circumstances, sir. My diver found your man, although I did not know that at the time I spoke to Captain Troughton." He addressed this to *Harwich*'s captain. "Your submarine, at least I presume it was *your* submarine, was picked up on our sonar while we were wreck-marking. My watch-officer would probably have ignored it, but you train your operators well. My quartermaster was a naval sonar operator some years ago. He recognised the sonar signature. It didn't take much to realise you were interested in the drums. Your," he nodded at Troughton again, "first lieutenant was pretty heated that I found most of them under the tarpaulin aft here. The label 'Dry-Cleaning Fluid' was clearly incorrect. You see gentlemen, you gave the game away by too many bluffs . . ."

"What do you mean *game*, Captain?"

Naismith sighed. He knew he was beaten, knew that if they wanted to they could, and would, get the truth out of him.

"Gentlemen, could we drop this pretence? It is obvious the stuff in the drum was more lethal than any industrial chemical I have ever heard of. It must destroy flesh in some way, even when diluted in several million parts of water. You do not kill men for lesser reasons, although you may have told my crew you did to save them all from a toxic substance, I don't know. But I do know the *Wallenstein* was bound for Santa Maria de los Mayas and the media tell me that around Santa Maria the countryside is being sprayed with nerve gas. They also tell me that the USA is supplying arms to the military junta in Santa Maria, but not even the media could pin nerve gas on Uncle Sam. So where does it come from, gentlemen?"

He sat back and watched the exchange of glances between the three men. The Rear-Admiral leaned forward and asked:

"Where do *you* suppose it originates, Captain?"

"An arms dump of the western alliance somewhere in West Germany, I imagine."

* * *

Naismith was conducted back to his cabin. He was left

206

to kick his heels for half an hour before being summoned to reappear before the "tribunal". He sensed a change in their attitude, a hardening of feature and tone of voice on the part of Hatchet-face, a more concerned look upon that of the Admiral. Troughton looked as though he had had some rough-handling from both of them.

"To how many other people did you make known your suspicions, Captain?" Hatchet-face asked.

"About the substance being nerve gas agent?" Hatchet-face nodded. "Nobody," he lied.

"Nobody? What about the telephone calls?"

"If you refer to my second officer's involvement," he said carefully, "you will find her concern with pollution much greater than mine, although," he shrugged with affected unconcern, "if she knew that it was nerve gas agent I daresay, being a woman, you would find her less tractable than myself . . ."

"Captain Naismith, are you saying that she didn't know it was nerve gas?" Troughton fired the question and earned a reproachful look from the Admiral and one of pure venom from Hatchet-face. It was an admission that he had been right and although it did not surprise him, it gave him a kind of comfort, like whisky hitting the pit of an empty stomach.

"I'm saying, gentlemen, that had she known it was a toxic chemical of *any* kind her reaction would have been exactly the same."

The Admiral and Hatchet-face put their heads together and Naismith realised that they had not monitored the content of the telephone calls except, perhaps, the last one in which nothing specific had been said. They had been able to trace Peter from the number recorded at the Telecom Satellite station at Goonhilly.

"Well, Captain," said Hatchet-face, "we are agreed. The matter was made too public to entirely hush up. It is therefore necessary that we remind you that you are a civilian employee of the Government and a signatory of the Official Secrets Act. I am sure it is not necessary to stress the powers that gives us. That is all Captain, for the present. Your superiors have been notified that *Active* and *Harwich* arrived at Spithead in company and that you will contact them in due course. For the time being you will remain on board *Harwich*."

"There is one question you have overlooked."

"What is that?" asked the Rear-Admiral.

"The man you shot."

Hatchet-face smiled coldly. "As you deduced Captain, we have explained to your crew the danger in opening the drum and that the man Davis seemed to be off his head. That it was in the interests of all of them that Davis was stopped doing what it appeared he intended to do."

Naismith swung round on Troughton. "Did *you* give the order?"

"No, Captain," went on Hatchet-face, "I did."

"And *you* have that power?"

"Oh, yes, Captain," Hatchet-face remarked quietly, "if the circumstances deem it necessary."

"Who *are* you?"

"That is not germane to these proceedings . . ."

"Then what about my seaman?"

"He has no relatives, Captain."

"But you are wrong. He has a wife living, or trying to live in Santa Maria de los Mayas."

Chapter Seventeen

"And then what happened?" Susan asked.

"It clearly had them rattled. I suggested large amounts of compensation might be claimed . . ." He broke off and sighed.

"Go on."

"Well it was no good. The Rear-Admiral told me in the end. The Hatchet-faced civilian wasn't in favour but the Admiral had decided I wasn't a bloody Bolshevik and did me the courtesy of an explanation."

"Go on," she said again.

"It seems that I'd got it wrong. I thought the stuff had come from a NATO arms dump, hence the British Government getting all excited and sending a destroyer to recover it. In a way it isn't as bad as all that, in a way it's far worse. I mean the British Government isn't the fly in the ointment . . ."

"Then who is?" There was an edge of impatience in her voice.

"Your friend Peter may find out through that German film maker, what was his name?"

"Harald, er, Harald Dietz."

"Yes. There is that firm, somewhere in Germany, that makes chemicals. This is a lucrative sideline, a spin-off which finds a market in the international arms trade. I mean why waste money on a nuclear bomb when you can get this stuff at a fraction of the price? Half the world's dictatorships will be queueing up for it. The admiral suggested the finance for this outfit is international. He mentioned our 'trans-Atlantic cousins'. The Germans have a certain reputation for poisonous gas," he said ironically.

"I still don't see why the Royal Navy had to get involved."

"Wheels within wheels, Susan, the price of freedom, and all that. Besides, they had lost a man on the wreck."

"Sorry, I don't understand."

"Well, the stuff *was* made in the West and right-wing elements in the West *were* supplying it to the junta in Costa Maya. Although no Western Government was directly involved; someone, somewhere must have known about it and rung the international alarm bells when the *Wallenstein* went down. The fact that it was financed and manufactured in the West would have been a propaganda coup for other, less friendly powers, wouldn't it? As the Rear-Admiral put it, recovery of the drums was in the interests of truth as much as anti-pollution. It would have been a lie, he said, to ascribe evil motives to HMG, however much we wanted to." Naismith laughed in the darkness. "I really don't think he comprehended our concern, you know: 'If any of this gets out it will be ascribed to the wrong motives. We will be blamed and that is why we were forced to take extreme measures,' he said."

"And you were satisfied?"

"No, not satisfied, but I believed the admiral. I remembered the logo on the drum. It was rather like the Legs of Man, a kind of swastika-like design . . ."

"And they let you go?"

"Yes, after a bit. They gave me the evening paper and sent me back as you know, in the admiral's barge. What happened aboard here?"

"Oh, after you'd gone it all simmered down. The drums and Davis disappeared very quickly via the helicopter, they pushed the crowd down below for that. Then the marines became all friendly and it was clear they had orders to make out nothing too irregular had occurred. There was lots of talk about it being a useful exercise for them, what a plucky fellow you were . . ."

"Huh! There must have been some reaction over Davis' death, for God's sake."

"Oh, there was, but it wasn't grief. Somebody suggested he'd been a bit queer ever since his son had died. That loudmouth Harris said he'd been a bit queer ever since he joined. (He fought Harris, you know, knocked him cold, I heard.) Young Ellice looked a bit cut up about it but when the marine officer told them all that if he hadn't been 'taken out', it was quite likely they would all have died from that *industrial* chemical, they seemed to accept it."

"That's unbelievable."

"It's a sign of the violent age we live in and the way we've become used to such things." She sighed. "Poor Davis. He would have opened that drum, you know."

"Yes, I know. What did he say to you?"

He heard the catch in her voice. "He said, 'I loved him, miss, I loved him and I'd never seen him. The bastards killed him first.' That's what he said, sir. Just before they blew his head off."

She spoke quite coolly and he could only guess at the effect witnessing Davis' death had had upon her. Perhaps she had already cried herself dry.

They both stared silently out over the dark sea as *Active* ploughed east, Beachy Head a pale blur in the night away on the port bow.

"Are we going to write and tell his wife? I found an address while I was gathering his things together."

"What happened to his personal effects?"

"They took them all ashore before you came back, but I copied the address."

"So poor Davis has become a non-person . . ."

"I'd like to write to her. His wife, I mean."

"Yes. Okay. You do that. What was Chas' reaction to it all?"

She shook her head in the darkness. "He thought you and I were having an affair I think."

"Good God!"

"Apparently he had seen me go into your cabin in the small hours. He was pretty mad about it. And he said I was insanely preoccupied with my campaign against pollution and that it had probably cost you your job and him his."

"What, because he hit me?"

"Yes."

"He looked quite astonished when I told him to forget it. I still don't think he understands even the official explanation of what went on." Naismith rubbed his sore jaw. "I shall have to tell him some of what happened."

They fell silent again, then she said, "They won, didn't they?"

Naismith smiled. "They were bound to really, Susan. God is always on the side of the big battalions."

"I thought I'd cured you of cynicism. I like to think it was more our little Masada, or Thermopylae. You know, 'Go tell the Spartans . . .'"

"Well the official line was quite plain," he said chuckling. "They held me in custody until after Prime Minister's Question Time. Haven't you seen the London evening paper they were at such pains to make sure I brought back to the ship with me?"

"No."

"The copy's on my desk. Go down and have a look at it."

She went below, entering Naismith's cabin. The *Evening Standard* lay open and the piece was marked. Her eyes adjusted to the light after the darkness on the bridge.

During Question Time in the Commons this afternoon the Prime Minister was asked if the Government was aware of any shipments of chemical weapons from Western Europe to any military dictatorships in Central America. He was also asked if there was any connection with newspaper allegations that the recent deaths of two fishermen after contact with polluted seawater were attributable to such substances being aboard a ship sunk recently off the Channel Islands. It was known that the ship was bound for Costa Maya where chemical warfare was being used against defenceless civilians.

The Prime Minister replied that such so-called news did the free-press great harm, that it was the result of journalistic wishful thinking and that the careless marriage of dramatic facts might make good copy but it did not make the truth.

The British Government's attitude to military dictatorships, particularly those in the Americas, was well known. The ship that sank was not British but had been carrying a toxic chemical and went down in waters over which Britain had a moral, if not a territorial, interest.

All the drums of this substance had been accounted

for after strenuous efforts by the Royal Navy and a ship of the British Navigational Aids Service, whose crews were deserving of the highest praise. As far as the Government was concerned, the Prime Minister assured the House, it had demonstrated its concern in preserving the waters around our coast from pollution.

"Clever isn't it?" said Naismith as Susan returned to the bridge. "A combination of truth and, er, veiled truth. So you see, the Spartans will never know what really happened."

They were silent for a long time, then at last Susan said, "With Peter's help I could tell them."

"Your Peter's got himself into enough trouble already. There's no way you can expose this sort of thing. They'd slap a 'D' Notice on it, or prosecute you under the Official Secrets Act, or something."

"No," she said with that note of inflexible determination in her voice that Naismith had learned to beware of. "No. I don't mean like that. I mean that between us we could write a book!"

"The literature of the Apocalypse, eh?" Naismith laughed cynically. "The trouble is, Susan, no one would believe it.

Epilogue

Susan sat in the Fleet Street pub and toyed with her gin and tonic. Outside the rain of a late December night slanted down, filthy with the passage of traffic as it splashed the pavements and threatened the forthcoming revels to see the New Year in.

The bar was crowded and she had already fended off two good-humoured advances as she struggled to keep Peter's place beside her. She saw him come in at last and smiled her relief.

"Sorry I've been so long," he said, smoothing his hair down and wiping the rain from his eyes.

"Did you get a copy?"

"Yes," he reached inside his raincoat and handed her the rolled newspaper. "It's in tomorrow's first editions, and Harald's picture is on the foreign news page."

Susan found what she was looking for and carefully scrutinised it. Peter ordered more drinks. "They are both there," he said.

"Yes . . . yes, I've found it." In the New Year's Honours, Captain Frederick Troughton, Royal Navy, was made a Companion of the Most Honourable Order of the Bath and Captain James Naismith of the British Navigational Aids Service was awarded an MBE.

"'Honours never fail to purchase silence', eh?"

quoted Peter, grinning sardonically over the rim of his whisky.

"But it's not fair! James Naismith succeeded where Troughton failed."

"Ah, but he'd been a naughty boy, besides BNAS doesn't have the cachet enjoyed by the Queen's Navee . . . Have a look at Harald's picture. At least the bastards didn't win."

Susan turned to the foreign news page.

The leading story was of the final overthrow of the military junta in Costa Maya after a fortnight's siege of the capital, Santa Maria. The final assault had seen some bitter fighting but the capture of the presidential palace had resulted in the declaration of a People's Republic.

"They don't seem to be able to make up their minds whether it's the big red bogeyman or whether it's a triumph for democracy," Peter said, nodding at the paper.

"No," she said, transferring her attention to the picture that was alongside the story. It was a dramatic photograph of the hoisting of the new Republic's flag over the presidential Palace in the final hours of the battle.

It was being hoisted by a young woman with a machine gun slung round her shoulder. She was very dark with the high cheekbones of indian ancestry, a wide mouth and a straight, Spanish nose.

"She's a cracker isn't she?"

"Yes," said Susan thoughtfully, "I wonder who she is?"

"The only real danger that exists is man himself . . . because we are the origin of all coming evil."

Carl Gustav Jung

"The only thing necessary for evil to triumph, is for good men to do nothing."

Edmund Burke